MW00979555

95

The
DELPHIC · CHOICE

Norma Johnston

Four Winds Press
New York

Four Winds Press
Macmillan Publishing Company
866 Third Avenue, New York, NY 10022
Collier Macmillan Canada, Inc.
First Edition
Printed in the United States of America

10   9   8   7   6   5   4   3   2   1

The text of this book is set in 12 point Simoncini Garamond.

Library of Congress Cataloging-in-Publication Data
Johnston, Norma.
The Delphic choice.
Summary: Visiting relatives in Turkey, Meredith
becomes involved in efforts to free her uncle, a hostage
negotiator for a Quaker peace mission, who is taken
hostage by an Islamic terrorist group.
[1. Hostages—Fiction. 2. Terrorism—Fiction.
3. Turkey—Fiction. 4. Quakers—Fiction] I. Title.
PZ7.J6453De   1989   [Fic]   88-24570
ISBN 0-02-747711-8

For Susan A. Wilder,
who researched it with me
in Istanbul

◊‖◊

The first time I heard about the Delphic choice was the first time I met Brandon Hurd—standing on the rocky path at Delphi with the dying sun behind him. The tour guide was herding our group along, and I lingered, waiting for Felicity to catch up with me.

She was making her way slowly up the steep, narrow path. Felicity—Aunt Felicity, really, my mother's much younger sister—was five months pregnant. She was also fiercely independent (since birth, according to my mother) and hated being hovered over. That's why I was pretending to go on ahead, even though I was traveling with her precisely because her husband, Mark, was convinced—with good reason—that she needed a companion for the duration.

Mark Greystoke was minding their two kids back in Istanbul, where he and Felicity had been living for the past three years. At the last minute, he hadn't been able to come to the States when Felicity did, to see my grandparents and some doctors and persuade my folks to let me go back with her. Mark worked with a Quaker peace mission in the Middle East, and as usual peace had become precarious at the worst possible time.

Nonetheless, it had been Mark, really, who'd persuaded

my folks to let me go to Istanbul. On the overseas telephone to my father's office, he'd told Dad what Felicity had not—that she'd had two miscarriages in the past two years and was in serious danger of having one this time, too. Mark had pointed out that since I'd just graduated from high school, two weeks after my seventeenth birthday, and since the whole family knew Dad was having an acute case of protective-fatheritis over the thought of me, Meredith Blake, off on my own in a coed dormitory, a semester's "foreign-exchange" visit with the Greystokes was an ideal solution. For all of us. I'd get the thrill of leaving home, which was in Bloomington, Illinois, for foreign glamour. Dad got the reassurance of my being chaperoned beneath a Quaker roof. Mark got the relief of knowing I'd keep Felicity from overdoing things, if necessary for her and the baby's health. Even though Turkey was a Muslim country, it wasn't an Arab one, Mark had pointed out. Meaning no threat of revolution. So to my surprised delight, my folks said yes.

And now here I was, standing on the steep path with the wind whipping my black hair in my eyes. The mountain air was thin, which explained why I felt slightly giddy. For the first time, I could understand why those ancient Greeks, in their mountaintop city-kingdoms, felt like gods. Everything was so sharp and bright, and distance was distorted. It seemed as if I could reach out my arms and touch the sky.

What I couldn't understand was why we had to be constantly marshaled and lectured to by an official guide. Ours looked like Melina Mercouri, the Greek movie star who was now an official in the Greek government, and she was every bit as domineering as a head of state.

"Agamemnon, Apollo, Achilles, Jason," I muttered beneath my breath. "Who cares about them, anyway?" Actually I did, a bit, but I was in no mood to be fair. "They couldn't even make up their minds what was right or wrong without a girl in a trance giving them the answer!"

"She didn't give them the answer," a voice said with faint condescension. "She gave them a lot of mumbo jumbo. She was stoned on the smoke coming through that crack in the rocks up ahead. They used to throw eucalyptus branches into it so the priestess would start speaking in strange tongues. But they always had some old man around to translate."

I pushed my hair out of my eyes and gave him a look. And then I looked again. He was gorgeous, with a Greek-god profile and dark blond hair and beard. But I was right about the condescension. My chin came up. "Some translations! You mean the most convenient political explanation. And even then they always gave their words a twist, so whatever the end result was, it fit the prophecy!"

His eyes, which had been going up and down me as if I were one of those statues in the Athens museum, sharpened with surprised respect. And, I couldn't help noticing, with admiration. I was glad I'd worn my embroidered Greek dress (it was too hot for jeans) and the earrings that were supposed to be authentic copies, in gold, of Clytemnestra's, and weren't really either.

"You're right," he said. "They had good reason to be ambiguous. They risked their necks if they weren't. But the point was, the ancient Greeks lived in a time of upheaval, and they needed the oracle to get them off the hook of the hard questions they were faced with. And their *hubris*—their pride, their fatal flaw—was that they weren't farsighted enough to recognize what the real issue was."

"I know what *hubris* means," I answered tartly. "What *was* the real issue?"

"How to choose between public duty and private duty. And the answer is that there *is* no answer." He smiled and strode down toward me, holding out his hand. "I'm sorry if I was obnoxious. But I'm sick of Agamemnon and Achilles and the other ancient Greeks being considered irrelevant and immaterial to modern life."

"Not here, they aren't."

He went on as if I hadn't spoken. "And sick of being condescended to as if I couldn't possibly know about them, or what I'm talking about."

I couldn't resist. "I know *exactly* what you mean."

He laughed. "*Touché.* Shall we shake and start over? I'm Brandon Hurd."

"Meredith Blake."

"Here on a study program?"

"No, on my way to the Middle East with my aunt. Are you?"

Brandon laughed briefly. "I'm on independent research. Translation: I couldn't find a job back home. The professors who'd talked me into getting my degree in Greek and Roman lit somehow never mentioned I'd wind up not qualified to do anything but type." His face took on a sheepish grin. "I graduated a year early, so I can take some time out before I go on with school."

"Me, too. High school, not college. That's why I'm taking a year out, part of a year, anyway."

"Why the Middle East? Particularly now?" Brandon asked. He dusted off a rock and sat, gesturing an invitation for me to do likewise.

"Because that's where my aunt and uncle live. I'm going to be their mother's helper till the new baby comes. What are you doing independent research for, your Ph.D.?"

"Yes," he said. "I got wise, though. I'm switching into political science. Particularly the roots of Arab-European conflict." I shivered, and Brandon gave me a shrewd look. "Speaking of which, I shouldn't think your uncle would want his wife and kids in the Middle East right now."

"They live in Istanbul. It's not as if it were in Tehran or Beirut. Anyway, you don't know my uncle! Mark Greystoke's something special."

Brandon started. "You don't mean that guy who's always going into hot spots and negotiating hostage releases! I'm flying to Istanbul myself tomorrow—I'd give my eyeteeth to meet him. I don't mean to be pushy, but do you think you could fix it up?"

I nodded, laughing. "I'm sure I could. He'd probably enjoy it, seeing the subject you've picked for your doctorate! Mark really is an expert. He's been involved with the peace movement ever since the sixties, when he was in high school. He's a genuine pacifist, and not out of cowardice or for political reasons. He's a Quaker. He's the one person I know who's totally without prejudice."

"You're not just a little bit prejudiced yourself, are you? About him, that is?" Brandon smiled.

"I guess I am. And you know what? I don't care."

5

We sat there companionably, as the flowery scents of Greek summer wafted over us. The sun sank lower. Off in the hyacinth-colored east was the first twinkle of the evening star.

And then, abruptly, the Delphic peace was broken. Felicity was stumbling toward us, panting, hurrying despite her condition and the doctors' warnings. She saw me and gasped out, "*Meredith*—"

I took one look and started to run, and Brandon ran also.

We caught her just as she stopped abruptly, then staggered and began to sway. Together we eased her down onto a rock.

Felicity's face was grayish yellow, and there were shadows beneath her closed eyes. My own heart pounded. I fanned her, and held her hand tightly, and after what seemed an eternity her eyelids fluttered.

"Don't try to talk," I said firmly. "Just breathe. Slowly." She obeyed, clinging to my hand. Her eyes were terrible. When she was calmer, I asked, "Felicity, what is it?"

"I just heard—on the radio in the shop. I recognized the names, and the storekeeper translated—"

"Nothing's happened to Mark?"

"No! Oh, no! But it's almost as if it had." Felicity drew a slow shuddering breath. "Stephen Althorp, a dear friend of ours and an Anglican priest, has been taken hostage. So has an American journalist we know. Snatched off the street, both of them."

"Who snatched them?" Brandon asked. "What's being asked for ransom?" Going straight to the important questions.

"Some Shiite splinter group. Militant. Nobody seems to have heard of them before, but there may be a tie with the P.L.O. No one seems to know yet why they were kidnapped."

"Where?" Brandon asked.

Felicity looked at Brandon vaguely. "What? Oh. Lebanon. Not in Beirut. In one of the smaller, disputed cities. Mark and I have been there. . . . The journalist's wife, she's Lebanese herself, she just lost a baby. . . ." Felicity turned to me.

"Meredith, I'm sorry. I've asked the shopkeeper to hire us a taxi—there are several hanging around down there. We've got to get back to the hotel at once. I want us on the first plane we can get to Istanbul. And I don't want to hear a word from you about my overdoing it! Stephen Althorp's Mark's closest friend. I know Mark will be going into Lebanon after him, and I have to see him first!"

·2·

The sunset colors had faded. There was just a soft rose glow in the west behind the rim of mountains. I stood there, feeling a light, chill breeze, and my heart was hammering. For an instant it was as if time had hurtled me back to ancient Greece, as if I were faint from the fumes of the Delphic fire and were reeling in horror from an oracle's words.

Only a minute, but it was so real. Then the sensation passed, and I was me, Meredith, my arms around Felicity, trying to dissuade her. I knew my words were driving Felicity frantic, but I couldn't stop.

Brandon's hand came down for a moment, firm, on one of mine. His voice, very calm and collected, said, "The taxi's probably waiting. Let's go on down."

Between us, he and I guided Felicity down the treacherous path. She was still weak and dizzy, but that steel will of hers sustained her. We reached the bottom and were back on fairly even flagstones. There were benches. "Want to sit for a minute?" Brandon asked. Felicity shook her head.

"We've got to get back—get packed. I want to leave tonight—"

My eyes and Brandon's met over Felicity's dark head

with a single thought. Brandon shook his head imperceptibly. *Better not now*, the nod said, and I agreed. Time
enough to fight out our departure schedule once we were
in our room at the Delphi hotel.

Felicity took a deep breath and her voice steadied. "I'm
all right." She took my arm and Brandon's, and we made
our way down the remaining walkway to the entrance
kiosk. A taxi waited there. Brandon helped Felicity and
me into the back seat, tipped the guard, then calmly
climbed into the front seat beside the driver. "You don't
mind if I bum a ride to my hotel, too, do you? Which one
are you staying at?" I told him, and he nodded. "Me, too.
That's convenient."

It was more than convenient, it was a godsend.
Brandon gave the driver the hotel name, with consider-
ably better Greek pronunciation than Felicity or I could
have managed. When we arrived he paid off the cab and
tipped the doorman, asking him to have coffee, mineral
water, and some fruit sent up to us at once. He escorted
us up to the door of our room and got the key to work,
which was more than I'd been able to do earlier.

"Thanks," Felicity said gratefully. "For everything.
Please come in and have some of that coffee with us,
Mr.—I don't even know your name—"

I supplied it, with a rapid explanation of how we'd met.
Felicity nodded. Now that we were back, her stamina was
beginning to desert her. "Mr. Hurd. You'll have to excuse
me—I've got to make arrangements—" She looked
around the cool blacks and whites of the hotel room
vaguely.

"I'll call the Athens airport for you, if you want." Brandon looked at me. "Excuse me for butting in, but it would be crazy trying to go back to Athens tonight. You couldn't possibly make the last flight, and those mountain roads are bad enough in daytime. I've already got a taxi lined up to drive me in the morning. You can ride with me."

"Fine," I said loudly, before Felicity could protest.

Brandon applied himself to the telephone, arguing in what sounded like mixed Greek and English. Finally he put down the receiver with a grin of triumph. "It's all set. You have two seats on the same plane I'm on, Olympic Airways' afternoon flight. We'll leave here right after breakfast and should reach Athens in time for lunch before boarding. Or we can stop at a *taverna* along the way if you'd rather."

Felicity didn't answer. She'd dragged out her suitcase and was just looking at it blankly. "I'll pack," I said. "You go lie down. Or take a shower."

There was a knock at the door—room service. Brandon answered it and took the tray from the waiter: bottled water and some chipped glasses; a bowl of fruit; thick Greek coffee in a copper pot with small cups in brass holders.

"I shouldn't," Felicity said, but she drank coffee anyway. It seemed to revive her. Brandon had coffee, too. I sipped mineral water. We sat around in a silence of mixed awkwardness and exhaustion.

"I think I will take that shower," Felicity said at last. She came over and gave Brandon her hand. "Mr. Hurd, I don't know how to thank you. All I can think of is to hope you'll be our guest for dinner."

"No thanks needed, but I'll be happy to accept." Brandon looked at me. "In the meantime I'm going for a swim. You feel like joining me?"

"I'll think about it."

"Good enough." He smiled at both of us, and left.

Felicity pulled off her embroidered Greek smock and lay down gratefully on her bed's black-embroidered rough wool spread. "You shower first. Then go swim. I'm fine, Mer; you don't need to hover."

She wanted to be alone, and she was probably going to try to reach Mark by phone. I showered, then put on my bathing suit and a violet-blue gauze caftan and went down to join Brandon Hurd at the hotel pool.

It was funny. I was still shaky, and I wasn't sure why. Or rather, I was sure it was no one thing. It was the news from Lebanon, bringing home to me as nothing had before just how dangerous life in the Middle East could be. And it was worry about Felicity, whom Mark and my parents had made my responsibility; Felicity, who always cared so much about other people that she was careless with herself. It was also that strange, almost mystical sensation of foreboding I'd felt there on the Delphic rocks. *And* it was the way Brandon Hurd made me feel.

I made my way to the hotel pool (half open to the moonlit night, half covered by the roof of the open-walled dining room) with considerable trepidation. And almost at once I knew I needn't have, that the silence in the room had been from old-shoe comfort, not awkwardness. As we swam and then lazed around the pool I felt as if Brandon and I had known each other forever.

"Do you believe in reincarnation?" I asked suddenly as we sat by the pool.

Brandon raised one golden eyebrow sardonically. "Don't tell me you're going to go mystic on me! I'm a scholar, remember? All scientific detachment."

"You know darn well the ancient Greeks believed in things like that," I retorted.

"They also believed in things like human sacrifice, in the early days, but that doesn't mean I have to. Or in the Fates!"

I just shrugged. We talked about everyday things after that, and eventually we went back to our rooms to dress for dinner.

Felicity was already dressed, in a caftan and sandals, her long dark hair knotted up with hairpins. She looked rested but grave. "Did you reach Mark?" I asked, and she shook her head.

"I couldn't make out whether the operator couldn't get a line through, or whether there was nobody home. Which doesn't make sense. Mark quite likely is running around trying to get word on Stephen, but the kids and the housekeeper should have been there. Unless the Farkases had them over for dinner. They're our next-door neighbors."

We had dinner in the open-air dining room, Felicity and Brandon and I; avgolemono soup and moussaka and bird's-nest pastries. Brandon was the only one who ate. Felicity just picked at her food, and I pushed mine around my plate. It had too much garlic and too much olive oil.

"I'm afraid you'll starve in Istanbul," Felicity said rue-fully. I said I'd manage, and Brandon said it wouldn't hurt me. It was just like we were all family. Almost, I forgot about that feeling of foreboding and the awful news about Mark's friend Stephen Althorp. Almost, that is, until I woke up in the small hours of the morning and found Felicity lying on the chaise lounge of our balcony, staring at the moon.

We left for Athens right after an early breakfast of bread and fruit and metal-tasting orange juice and thick, bitter coffee. The trip was awful. It wasn't just that the road was steep and narrow and clung to the sheer edge of the cliffs. The taxi was ancient; the driver spoke no English. We corkscrewed and spiraled, lurching this way and that. Twice, oxcarts passed us, coming from the opposite direc-tion. A few times tour buses overtook us, the passengers' faces pressed against the window glass. Felicity's face was first white, then gray. My heart was in my throat. I'd heard that expression all my life and always thought it corny, but I didn't anymore.

At noon Brandon twisted round in the front seat to face us. "Want to stop for lunch?"

Felicity shook her head. I cleared my throat. "How much farther?"

"About an hour at the rate he's driving. Want to wait till we get to Athens? We can go to the Hilton and get plain old American food." I nodded fervently, and Brandon laughed. So that's what we did, ate in the quiet, umbrella-shaded peace of the Hilton's pool terrace where the flagstones felt as unsteady as if we'd just stepped off a lurching boat.

Halfway through the meal Felicity pushed back her chair and excused herself. I half-rose, wondering if she were ill, but her eyes signaled me to stay. She went inside and returned five minutes later, her face rock stern. She was carrying a copy of the *International Herald Tribune.*

Hostage Lives in Jeopardy, screamed the English head-line.

Brandon and I grabbed the paper as she flattened it on the table. There were pictures of Stephen Althorp (at a recent Anglican conference in London), of the American journalist (smudged photo) and of the car (bullet riddled) from which the journalist had been dragged in an ambush. The group or groups responsible for the kidnap-pings had not yet been identified; no group was taking credit; no ransom request had been received. Washington was demanding immediate action, and London was coun-seling calm.

"We should flex some military muscles," Brandon said grimly.

"That's not what Mark would say," I said automatically. And then I wondered. Stephen Althorp was Mark's best friend. But Felicity was nodding.

"We shouldn't be hasty. Nations have to reason together—*people* have to. The splinter groups, the funda-mentalists, they have grievances too."

"How can you reason with terrorists? Especially when you don't even know—" Brandon stopped. "I think we'd better be getting to the airport."

We paid the bill and left.

Athens seemed so calm, sleeping in the midday sun. So did the airport, all white and blue and modern. We turned our luggage over to a porter, reported to the Olympic Airways desk, and picked up tickets, seat assignments, and boarding passes. Then, as we walked toward the departure gate, I looked across the marble length of the terminal, and a fist seemed to close inside my throat.

There were soldiers with machine guns at all the gates.

There were soldiers with machine guns at the elevators and the exits.

I turned, shocked, to Felicity, but her face was undisturbed. *She's seen all this before*, something inside me whispered. I felt sick. Brandon frowned. But when we reached our gate the soldiers just stood like statues. The mixed bag of passengers (all kinds, all ages) sat stoically in the waiting area. Time passed. The air grew blue with cigarette smoke.

"We made it in plenty of time after all," Brandon murmured to me in an undertone, and I whispered back, "Thanks to a cab driver who thought he was in an airplane!"

More time went by, and nothing happened. A baby cried; restless children ran around. Felicity watched them quietly. Brandon sat reading a Robert Ludlum thriller. He looked over the top of it to me and grimaced. Then he straightened.

"Looks like some activity's going to take place," he murmured. Four uniformed Olympic Airways personnel came in, carrying small black cases like tape recorders. They began walking purposefully between the rows of seats, and at first I was puzzled. Then I realized the cases were some kind of sensor devices, and I shivered.

Finally, they left. Two uniformed men wearing pilot's

wings appeared and strode past us, heading for the plane. They disappeared. The door to the tube leading to the plane opened again. A loudspeaker squawked, first in Greek, then in some other language, then in English. "Now boarding Olympic Airways. . . ." We all rose thankfully, gathering our carry-on junk. Flight attendants checked our boarding passes, steered us to our seats. Brandon was in another section, behind Felicity and me. "See you in Istanbul," he said cheerfully as he passed us.

We settled ourselves and buckled our seat belts. Sunlight streamed in the windows and dazzled on the metal outside. The plane was stuffy, with the air conditioning not yet turned on. At last the door was shut, the attendants seated themselves, and the power began to hum. The plane began to taxi slowly out onto the field. It was a moment that never failed to fill me with a mixture of elation and apprehension. I looked at Felicity with a half smile, but Felicity's eyes were closed. There were still shadows underneath her eyes.

We circled, awaiting takeoff clearance. The air conditioning had started on, one jet of it aimed right at my neck. There was a whoosh of rushing air, as if the plane were gathering forces for a burst of speed.

And then the whoosh stopped. The plane stopped, on the far side of the field. The air conditioning went off. That means the motor's turned off, something inside me said. My earlier apprehension became a worm that twisted in my stomach.

We sat. The flight attendants disappeared into the cockpit, and outside the window the sun glittered on the metallic gray of the flying field, the yellow-gray-white of ground and hills beyond, the silvery green-gray of olive trees. The air grew close and hot, and we sat.

And then there were sirens outside, coming from the terminal. There were military trucks, and soldiers with camouflage suits and machine guns spilling out to surround us. The cockpit door opened, and the door to the plane. Then the flight attendants were hurrying down the aisle, speaking in staccato, excited Greek, almost pulling and pushing us toward the door and the hastily brought-up flight of steps, down onto the sun-baked tarmac.

·3·

It was happening too fast to comprehend. I know I grabbed my purse, and Felicity's, and I know I tried to help Felicity down the steps. Felicity was in a kind of trance. We were herded into about five groups far over on the tarmac, each group surrounded by gun-carrying guards. Felicity sat down on the tarmac, cross-legged, her hands folded quietly and her eyes closed. All I could think was, My God, we've been taken hostage.

A hand touched my shoulder and I almost screamed. It was Brandon, murmuring with measured calm, "Don't worry, it's not what you think."

"What—"

Before I could go on, he had me in his arms and was nuzzling my neck below my ear. What he was really doing was whispering. "The soldiers are Greek army. They're trying to keep things hushed up, but from what I could make out there's been a report of a bomb on board. Stay cool."

He released me, with a smile belied by the worry in his eyes. I looked around. The belly of the plane was open, and laborers were unloading all the luggage. It stood around in the white glare and looked forlorn.

After what seemed an eternity, airport security officials

began to move among us. One person from each party traveling together was sent to locate our group's luggage and stand by while it was searched. Searched thoroughly and completely, with the electronic sensors I'd seen earlier. Some objects, some bags were confiscated . . . none of them ours, to my profound relief. Then, one by one, we were left to repack our private possessions publicly displayed. Brandon was philosophic, Felicity resigned. I felt angry and embarrassed as I stuffed belongings back into suitcases, and the worm of apprehension in my stomach began to grow. For all my keeping up with the news, all my pacifist convictions, I *hadn't* understood what life in the Middle East—even near the Middle East—was like.

After another apparent eternity, we were put through intensive examination of our passports and cross-examination as to destination and purpose of our travel. "I'm visiting my aunt and uncle," I said.

The officer's eyes were skeptical. "For several months?"

"Yes. I'm going to be a—a mother's helper." Let them figure out the Greek translation of that, I thought.

"Your aunt is not able to find servants in Istanbul?"

"She wants a relative with her. She's pregnant," I said acidly. Felicity, fortunately, was being interrogated by someone else and didn't hear.

"So. Your aunt is with you? But your uncle is not here?"

"He couldn't come. My aunt is over there." I saw the officer look Felicity over thoughtfully. I supplied Mark's name, and our Istanbul address. At last we were both allowed to board the plane.

Soon after, Brandon came squeezing down the aisle to sit in the seat across from mine. I raised my eyebrows, and he said calmly, "I've arranged a seat change." I was gladder than I wanted him to see. There was something ordinary and reassuring about the way he sat there, reading the thriller he'd picked up in the airport.

The plane's power and air conditioning started up again, and at last we were taxiing down the runway for real and taking off into a sky in which the sun was already low in the west. The flight seemed endless. Felicity said little, but I could sense a deep disquietude in her. She gazed unseeingly out the window or at a magazine, or dozed. Brandon and I played chess on his pocket-sized folding chessboard. Flight attendants began rattling dinner carts. Our trays came, and there was more moussaka, oily and heavy. I just picked at mine, and Felicity didn't even try.

Dessert was fresh figs and oranges, and Brandon took out a pocketknife and peeled them for us. When we'd finished, I looked at my sticky fingers ruefully. "I'd better wash."

"There's a long line for the bathrooms already," Brandon pointed out. We joined it anyway. I got one first and washed with difficulty in the cramped cubicle. My face stared back at me from the mirror like a stranger's face in the dim light, wan and dark-circled. I splashed water on it, braided my hair up to get it off my neck, and squeezed back out. Brandon was nowhere to be seen, and the waiting line was even longer. I squeezed past it down the narrow aisle.

Felicity was still sitting as I'd left her. I started to hurry toward her, smiling. And then I stopped.

A man walking ahead of me down the aisle had stopped

beside our seats and was bending over toward Felicity. I saw her eyes widen. Then he was gone, disappearing into the next cabin. All I could remember about him was the European cut of his dark suit and the curly blackness of his hair.

I slid into my seat, asking Felicity, "Who was that?" and found my voice was hoarse.

Felicity shook her head as if to clear it. "Someone I must have met somewhere. I don't remember."

"Then what makes you think you met him?"

Her eyes widened again. "He called me by name."

My heart was starting to pound. "What did he want?"

"I don't know," Felicity said vaguely and turned away.

I stared at her, sitting with deliberate stillness with her eyes closed and a little pulse pounding in her temple. Another picture leaped into my mind. Myself on the tarmac, being cross-examined by the official . . . pointing out my aunt, identifying her as Mark Greystoke's wife.

All I could think of was the man I'd seen with Felicity, the man whom she hadn't recognized but about whom she'd lied. And about Mark Greystoke—pacifist, activist, hostage negotiator, whose friend had been taken hostage.

I was here to protect Felicity from stress and worry, and somehow I had failed. I certainly wasn't here to disturb her with my probing. But I decided that I was going to speak to Mark about the stranger as soon as we reached Istanbul. Before he left; before he could come up with a way of turning my questions away with a soft answer.

◇ 4 ◇

A voice spoke suddenly beside me. "What happened?" Brandon was staring at me. "You look like somebody just walked over your grave."

"Don't say stuff like that!" I said sharply.

"Okay, I won't." Brandon studied me closely, but just said, in a perfectly ordinary tone, "Want to play some more chess?"

So we did. Felicity drowsed off. When our game ended, she was sound asleep.

The flight attendants were collecting empty plastic cups and stowing the beverage cart away. The pilot's voice came, indistinguishable in static, through the intercom. Brandon stretched and put away his chess set. "We're almost there," he said.

Around us in the airplane, people began to stir. Felicity stretched and returned her seat to its upright position. "Were you able to get some sleep, Meredith? I did. Look, honey, down to our right. That's the Galata Bridge and the Golden Horn—gateway between the Western World and the Middle East."

I looked dutifully out the window. The sky was pitch black, and far below lights sparkled like a hundred diamond necklaces. "It must be midnight. I hope there are taxis," Felicity murmured.

Extinguish cigarettes—fasten seat belts signs flashed on in Greek and English. My ears were popping. With a whoosh and a rush, the plane set down and taxied around to draw up near what looked like a set from an old movie.

There was no tube from the plane door into the terminal, only a set of stairs. We climbed down onto tarmac, as we'd done in Athens, but this time no uniformed guards were hovering. Luggage was being unloaded onto trucks, and passengers picked their way toward the terminal through soft, hot darkness interrupted by warm breezes and faint pools of light.

I shouldered my carry-on and, after one look at Felicity, took hers, too. "Come on, let's get out of here," I said firmly. With me on one side of her, Brandon on the other, we headed for the terminal.

It was huge, and dilapidated, and eerie, like an enormous Quonset hut left over from World War II. Exposed framework like Erector sets; rickety luggage conveyor belts; dark, robed men of undeterminable ages, gold toothed or gap toothed, moving cartons and cases, but none available to help us with our luggage; here and there obviously wealthy men and women in European clothes and gold and diamond jewelry.

Brandon was looking at us with a touch of alarm and saying, "We'd better get you two home before you come unglued." He took command of us and our luggage and I was never so glad to surrender responsibility to anyone. My main concern was Felicity, who was moving like a sleepwalker with the precarious control I recognized all too well. Why hadn't I tried phoning Mark from the Athens airport? Why hadn't I sent a telegram, so Mark could have had us met—or come himself? I realized, with a sudden, sharp stab, just how much I was aching to see my uncle.

Customs and immigration formalities were perfunctory. Felicity had a resident alien's visa, and the official examined it closely but made no comment if her name rang any bells. My passport was stamped almost without being looked at, and so was Brandon's. Our luggage was waved through without being opened. Then we were out at the great gaping entrance of the terminal, feeling the breeze against our bare skin and trying in vain to find a taxi.

Finally one pulled up before us. I tried explaining the address to the driver, first in English and then in French, but the old man just shook his head. Then Felicity dragged herself out of her daze and said something or other in Turkish. The driver nodded and reached an arm back to open the rear door, and Felicity and I climbed in. Brandon loaded the luggage while the driver sat smoking a foul-smelling cigarette, and then got in beside him. With a screech of gears and a jolting of broken shock absorbers, we took off.

It wasn't till then, when I could at last sit back, that something stirred inside me. A thread of—what? Doubt? Alarm? I didn't know, and because I was weary it wasn't very strong, but as we jounced along toward the lights of Istanbul a question began jouncing in my brain. If the Golden Horn was the gateway between the Western world and the Middle East, why was security at the airport so casual?

The lights along the road grew brighter and closer together. Low to our right was the ripple of water, and ahead the twinkling lights of skyscrapers on the hillside, like a medieval city in a fairy tale. More lights on the farther shore, and great domes, and slender minarets silvered by faint moonlight. And spanning the water, like a silver scimitar, jewel-gleaming—

"Stamboul," our driver said, waving his right arm proudly. "Stamboul" was the ancient, still-used name for Istanbul. "Galata Bridge."

My throat caught, and I heard Felicity laugh softly.

Brandon turned around in the front seat to face her. "Is it okay if the driver leaves me off first?" he asked apologetically. "I don't have much faith in where he'd dump me out if I tried to tell him where I'm going."

"Yes, of course." Felicity blinked. "Or we can put you up for the night. . . ."

"There's no need. I have a hotel reservation." Brandon named the hotel, and Felicity repeated it in Turkish for the driver. It was one of those places described in guidebooks as "plain, respectable, clean, suitable for students."

"Sure you won't change your mind?" Felicity asked dryly when we pulled up to the hotel and she saw Brandon's face.

He shook his head. "Not unless I could be of help to you. If it's okay, I'll call you tomorrow to see how you both are."

It was I who nodded. Felicity fished in her purse for her card, printed both in English and in Arabic, and passed it to him. Brandon got out, pulled out his suitcase, and headed for the hotel door. The taxi jolted off before he reached it.

We left the cheap tourist district and went toward the

river. No, not a river . . . vague memories from books I'd read before leaving home drifted back into my drowsy mind. Istanbul lay on the Bosphorus, that narrow strait connecting the Sea of Marmara on the west with the Black Sea on the east. The city itself was on both shores, though the Asian side wasn't as densely populated; most of the historical sites, and the more modern, international part, lay on the European side. The Galata Bridge connected the new part with the old city on the Golden Horn. The slender point of land formed one of the most fabled harbors in the world.

Mark and Felicity lived in the international quarter, near Taksim Square, in a quiet residential area popular with mid-level executives and professional people. There were palm trees, and buildings shouldering on the street but closed and indrawn, with few windows. Felicity was leaning back in the seat, her eyes closed, and I wondered how much farther we had to go. Then, with a final rattle, the taxi stopped.

We were in front of a square building of plain stucco, drab tan in the faint light. The few barred windows facing the road were shuttered, and the door was also barred. It looked deserted. I glanced at Felicity with something like alarm, and Felicity's eyes struggled open.

"Are we there? My keys are in my purse somewhere . . . on a silver ring."

I found them. I found Felicity's billfold, and some Turkish money, and paid the driver, hoping I wasn't overpaying exorbitantly. I got out, and got Felicity out—literally, for she was hugging her stomach and there was a pinched look around her nose and mouth. A tremor of fear ran through me. *The baby* . . . the baby, and Felicity's past history, and that awful bumpy ride. There wasn't time to think about it now. I propped Felicity against the doorframe, got our luggage with no help from the driver, and began an assault on the door with bell and keys.

Nobody came. No lights went on, and the alarm inside me grew and grew. At last I felt the key turn. The door swung open, and I steered Felicity inside.

We were in a small oblong room, tile floored, opening onto a central atrium. Its roof, three stories up, was open to the sky, and the scent of perfume and the splash of water came from a flower-circled fountain.

I didn't know where to find the lights. I got Felicity down on a bench. "Mark!" I called.

There was no answer.

I called again, *"Mark!"* Called loudly, and heard nothing but my own voice echoing and the splashing fountain. And then, far up, an arrow of light came as a door somewhere opened. A figure appeared on the uppermost gallery. A female voice called something sharply in a foreign tongue, and I shouted back. "It's Felicity Greystoke and Meredith Blake! Somebody come here quickly!"

I heard a gasp, and then light flooded down into the atrium from hanging lanterns. A girl came running down the wrought-iron stairs that linked the galleries. She was in her nightgown, and she had red-gold hair. She was Turkish, I was sure of that as she came closer, but her English was accentless and perfect.

"Felicity—praise Allah! We called the hotel in Delphi

but couldn't reach her." The girl looked past me, saw Felicity, and her eyes darkened with alarm. "What happened?" she demanded.

It was no time for niceties. "I don't know, but she's in bad shape. Where's Mark? And who are *you?*"

"Amina Farkas. I live next door. I came over to stay with the children because Fatma's sick." Fatma, I knew, was the housekeeper. "Mark's gone."

I stared at her blankly. "What do you mean *gone?*"

Amina shook her head. "We don't know. Fatma called my mother hours ago, and she was frantic. Mark just didn't come home, and he'd called earlier and told her particularly to have dinner ready at seven o'clock and to keep the children waiting to eat with him. He didn't come, and she couldn't get any answer at his office. What she did get was two phone calls with the caller hanging up as soon as she spoke into the receiver. Fatma's absolutely convinced Mark's been kidnapped."

·5·

Involuntarily, I gasped aloud. At once Felicity's voice came, sharp with anxiety. "Meredith? Are you all right? What is—" Her voice changed. "*Amina?* What's going on? The children?"

Amina and I exchanged glances. "They're fine," Amina said with admirable calm. "Fatma's having some of her stomach trouble again, is all. And it's Kamil's night to go home to his family, so Mama said I should come stay here. In case the children woke in the night or anything." She went quickly to Felicity. "Mrs. Greystoke, are you well? Should I call my mother?"

Felicity shook her head. "I'll be fine, once I get in my own bed. It's been a rough two days. Isn't Mark here?"

Again Amina's glance, dark with warning, caught mine. But she said merely, "Mr. Greystoke hasn't come home. Apparently some business . . . Miss—Blake, did you say? If you will help me take your aunt upstairs—"

"How many times do I have to tell you a pregnant lady is not a basket case?" Felicity interrupted wearily. "If you two and Fatma hover like this for the next four months I'll be stir crazy before the child is born! So Mark hasn't shown up, and Fatma's convinced again he's been snatched by terrorists, am I right?"

I gaped, Amina avoided her eyes, and Felicity laughed. "I *am* right. Oh dear, it's really wicked of me, but I'm glad Fatma's sick in bed. Arguing with her dire predictions at this hour would be all I need."

She started slowly for the staircase, hugging her stomach as she did so. The light from the hanging lanterns, high above us, threw her shadow, oddly distorted, against the wall. Her face looked gray in the yellow light, and worry pricked me.

"Shouldn't we . . . try to find out where Mark is?" I asked hesitantly.

"I know where he is. He's gone to look for Stephen Althorp and that journalist, of course. So much for my trying to get here before he took off." Felicity hauled herself up a couple of steps, then bent forward with a little cry and eased herself gingerly down onto the next step. "Amina—maybe you had better phone your mother."

Amina vanished into one of the rooms opening off the atrium. I sat down beside Felicity swiftly. "What is it? Shouldn't we call a doctor?" My voice was growing shrill.

"*Hush.*" Felicity caught my wrist. "Don't wake the children," she whispered. "Old Fatma will have scared them enough already, and there's no need."

"Felicity, are you sure?"

"Yes, I'm sure. Amina's mother *is* a doctor—oh, there she is," Felicity broke off with relief as the doorbell shrilled.

Amina ran to the door, and after that everything was out of my hands. A striking woman with red-gold hair like Amina's and a trenchcoat belted over her nightgown hurried in, followed by two strong-looking manservants.

Within minutes they had Felicity in a chair-lift in their arms and were carrying her up the stairs. Amina and I hurried ahead to turn down her bed. Felicity was laid down on white sheets smelling of sandalwood. Dr. Suni Koc—somewhere in all this, Amina managed to make formal introductions—pulled a blood-pressure cuff and stethoscope out of her medical bag.

"How long has your aunt been acting as if she's in pain?" she demanded.

I started to tell her, over Felicity's weak protests. Then running footsteps began to pound above our heads.

"The children—" Felicity started in alarm. Dr. Koc pushed her back down.

"I'll keep them away. Don't worry." I hurried out, shutting the door behind me.

Matt and Rachel were on the upper gallery. They took one look and flung themselves toward me. "Meredith!" "When did you guys get here? Where's Mom?"

"Shh! She's gone to bed; she was tired." I ran to meet them and turned them back upward firmly. There would be bustle going on around Felicity's room, and Felicity didn't want the kids upset. "How about you two showing me where I'm going to sleep?"

"You're up here next to me. Fatma was going to put you in the best guest room down below, but we wouldn't let her." Ten-year-old Rachel slid an arm around my waist and hugged me hard. She had long dark hair like her mother's, and dark gold eyes like mine.

"Fatma's silly," Matt said with scorn. He was two years younger, and he stared at me with gray-brown eyes so like his father's that I almost shivered. Suddenly he butted me in the stomach with his head. That was his way of showing affection since he decided he was too old for hugging. I hugged him anyway.

"What do you mean Fatma's silly?" I asked.

Matt shrugged. Rachel lifted her eyebrows gravely. "Go back to sleep, Matt," she ordered. "*I'm* taking care of Meredith."

Matt made an awful face, but he obeyed. Rachel escorted me into a small, high-ceilinged room with a brass bed and beautiful Persian rugs. "This is your room. If you wait till morning, Kamil will bring your suitcase up. You won't need your nightgown. Mom always keeps caftans in the armoire for unexpected guests."

"That will be fine," I said carefully.

Rachel was already getting one out, deep-blue crinkled cotton trimmed with white crochet. She turned down the bed in the same formal, grown-up manner. "I knew you guys would get back tonight," she said, folding the embroidered spread.

"Oh?"

"Because Daddy went to Lebanon."

"How did you know that?" I asked, trying to be equally casual. I meant both where Mark had gone and our return.

Rachel gave that little eyebrow lift again. "He always goes where something happens. Especially when it's to a friend. Fatma thinks Daddy's been kidnapped," she said disdainfully. "Matt's right, she is silly." Suddenly she spun round and flung herself at me in another bear hug. "Meredith, I'm glad you came!"

"I am too, sweetie." I hugged her tightly. "Want to stay

in here with me for what's left of the night?"

Rachel shook her head, heaving a deep sigh. "It'd be just like Fatma to decide to come up and check on us. If she found my bed empty she'd make a fuss. See you in the morning, Mer." She trailed out, hiding a yawn.

I stood in the doorway for a moment, looking after her. There were murmurs of voices coming from below, then the sound of the front door opening and closing. The manservants going? And Dr. Koc as well? I wanted to go down to Felicity, but was afraid that could be wrong.

I went back into my room, closing the door behind me quietly.

The room was tranquil, bearing the stamp of both Felicity and Mark. A Byzantine icon picturing a Madonna and Child hung on the wall above the bed. . . . Back in the fourth century, when Istanbul was called Byzantium, the Roman emperor Constantine had seen the sign of the cross in the sky and won a war with that sign on his standards and been converted to Christianity: "In this sign conquer." Constantine renamed Byzantium, calling it Constantinople, and made it his capital. I'd learned about that in world history class. How many wars had been fought for holy causes, and how many warriors, of many different faiths, had been convinced God was on the side of them and their religion?

I wasn't going to think about that now, for it made me think about Mark, and about Stephen Althorp and the American journalist, who were hostages in what the kidnappers probably also considered a holy war. If I thought about it, I wouldn't get to sleep, and I'd be a mess tomorrow, when Felicity would need me to be strong.

Had Mark gone underground? To Lebanon? Why was Rachel so sure of that? Why was Felicity so sure?

The shutters were closed at the double window. I undressed, splashing my face with water from a blue-and-white china pitcher on the washstand. I was dusty from travel, but I'd survive till morning, when I could find a bathroom and a shower. All at once I was so tired I ached. I dropped my clothes on a carved dark chair and stared through sleep-fogged eyes at my reflection in the brass-framed mirror above the chest of drawers. My face looked pale, drawn, my black hair falling out of its looped-up braid. A face above an unfamiliar caftan. Distorted, some-how, like an image in an icon.

I went to the window and opened the bars of the shutters wider. A faint breeze came in, bringing the scent of unfamiliar flowers. There were heavy, intricately wrought black iron bars on the outside of the windows. At least nobody could get in.

What had made me think that?

I shivered, not from cold. Felicity had been right; this had been a very unsettling two days. I climbed into bed, and put out the bedside lamp, and lay in the dark with my arms locked behind my head.

I was so weary that my head was loopy, like those old-time priestesses at Delphi getting high on eucalyptus smoke. But I couldn't sleep. I lay there in a kind of half-sleep, while disconnected images floated through my head.

Presently there was a soft tap on the door.

"Who is it?" I called quietly.

"Amina Farkas. May I come in?"

"The door's unlocked," I answered, and Amina slipped in, closing the door behind her.

"Mama and I are leaving now. Mama says your aunt is asleep." Amina sat down on the edge of my bed. "I thought you would want to know, Mrs. Greystoke was bleeding very slightly, but it has stopped now. The baby does not seem to be in present danger. Mama will talk to Mrs. Greystoke's obstetrician in the morning." Amina hesitated. "Miss Blake—"

"Meredith."

"Meredith." Amina smiled, but her eyes were grave. "My mother did not tell me to say this, but I am going to all the same. You will have to be firm with Fatma. She must not be allowed to upset Mrs. Greystoke, or the children."

"You mean about my uncle?" I asked deliberately.

Amina nodded. "I know your aunt believes he has gone underground into Lebanon, to bargain with the terrorists for his friend's release. She believes she received a message from him saying so. Someone on the plane whispered a blessing to her in Arabic, *Bismillahi ar rahman ar rahim.* 'In the name of Allah, the merciful, the compassionate.' It is the prayer used before starting on a journey."

I nodded and waited, sensing more to come. Amina paused, one finger tracing a spiral on the bedsheet. Suddenly she looked me straight in the eyes.

"I do not wish to alarm you, but those telephone calls Fatma answered, the ones with no one there . . . Mrs. Greystoke is sure they were from friends in the underground network Mr. Greystoke calls 'the peacemakers.' My mother feels it is best to allow her to go on believing so. But I must tell you that such calls are the way some terrorist groups signal that an attack is coming, or how they check on the whereabouts of someone they are seeking."

"How do you know that?" I whispered hoarsely.

"I just know, that's all," Amina said vaguely. She started to say something more, and stopped.

I sat up quickly. "Amina, what is it? If there's more, you have to tell me."

"There were threats," Amina said at last. "Since your aunt's been gone, before Mr. Greystoke's friend was taken. Mr. Greystoke received threats. That's all I can tell you."

She rose and, before I could stop her, slipped out. Moments later, I heard the heavy front door open and close.

· 6 ·

In the morning I was awakened early by the smell of strong Middle Eastern coffee and the sounds of *muezzins*, or criers, giving the call to prayer. The second of the "Five Pillars of Islam" and the Muslim faith's most important duty: "Homage to God, and acknowledgment that from God comes our life and all that we possess. One bedrock belief that the Muslim and Judaic and Christian faiths have in common." I could almost hear Mark's voice explaining that to me, two Christmases ago, the last time I'd seen him, when the Greystokes had been home on stateside leave.

I had answered that it was so darn stupid the way the whole world concentrated on the *differences* between people rather than the *samenesses*. Mark had sighed as though he agreed. Then he'd straightened with a smile. "I wouldn't have much faith either if I let myself get hung up being angry about that, would I?" he'd said to me, eyes twinkling.

"I don't know how you keep from it," I'd said darkly. I'd been remembering how we'd all watched the TV news on Christmas Eve, and the sharp contrasts that our minister had spoken of later at midnight service. Streams of worshipers at St. Patrick's Cathedral in New York and St.

Peter's Square, and Bethlehem; bloodshed in the Middle East. Glittering store windows with last-minute shoppers; the homeless at soup kitchens or sleeping on the streets. And, as always, stories of crime and death, of peace negotiations and terrorism, and rumors of little wars.

After we'd come home from church and had cookies and hot spiced cider, after Matt and Rachel were in bed, my grandparents and parents and I and Mark and Felicity had sat up talking. My grandfather, as protective of Felicity as Dad is of me, had come out all ex-marine, recommending "bashing their heads together" (their being anybody whose beliefs differed from his own down-home ones) and saying it was high time Mark and "the rest of you do-good fellers" woke up to what the world was really like.

Gran had pressed her lips together, and Mother had given me a warning glance. But Mark had laughed. Mark had said believing with your eyes shut was no belief at all, and personally he had his wide open, and that's why he still had faith. Gramp had grumbled that Mark would feel differently if anything affected him personally. Gran had changed the subject by pointing out that it was almost dawn.

It was almost dawn now, and Gramp's words were coming back all too vividly. Was something affecting Mark personally right now, or was I getting spooked?

I just hoped he *had* gone looking for the kidnapped men as Felicity had asserted; that he hadn't been abducted himself. Especially not now, when Felicity—*Felicity!* I jumped up wondering what was happening downstairs. And at that moment my bedroom door burst open and Rachel rushed in.

"*Mer,* thank goodness you're up! Come quick!"

"What's happened—Felicity—"

"Mom's okay," Rachel interrupted. "But she won't be if Fatma gets hold of her." She dashed down the stairs and I followed, my caftan billowing out behind me.

Matt was plastered across Felicity's closed door, his arms outstretched, glaring defiantly at a tall, black-garbed figure. A stooped, elderly man in a worn robe was trying to pull the woman away, and both were shouting. The words I couldn't understand, but the tone was all too clear. Suddenly the woman's right arm swung out, knocking the man off balance. Matt screamed, and she reached for his shoulder. And I shouted.

"*Stop it!* All of you!" They stopped as if frozen, and turned to face me. I went on down the stairs, slowly and grimly.

"Madame Greystoke is ill. She is not to be disturbed by anything. *Anything!* Do you understand me?" My voice came out as I wanted it to, low and stern. Fatma stared at me. I'd have known she was Fatma, even without Rachel's saying so, from the gold tooth and leather skin I'd heard about for years. She was Matt's nurse when he was a baby and now was housekeeper and thought she owned the place. I stared back at her implacably, though I shook inside.

"I am Miss Blake. Mr. Greystoke has charged me to look after Mrs. Greystoke and the children until his return. She must have rest and peace. If anything happens to disturb her, or hurt the child she's carrying, it will be on your head. Do you understand me?"

I sounded melodramatic, but it worked. Not taking her eyes from me, Fatma nodded.

"Good," I said less forcefully. "Now please take the children down and give them breakfast, and send some bread and fruit up to Madame's room."

To my relief, they all obeyed me, Rachel shooting me a look of respect and triumph as they left. I took a deep breath and opened Felicity's door.

Felicity was sitting up in bed laughing at me.

"What was that all about? Fatma pushing the Portents of Doom button?" she inquired.

I blushed. "Felicity, you were listening!"

"I was, and you did us proud. Just what the doctor and my husband ordered! Meredith, I am glad you're here."

"So am I, all things considered," I said. "Oh, no, you don't!" Felicity was swinging her feet over the edge of the bed. I pushed them back firmly. "Shouldn't you stay in bed?"

"As a matter of fact, Suni did think I should stay in bed till my obstetrician looks me over." Felicity grimaced, but she let me tuck her in. "I'm fine! The scare yesterday was a false alarm."

"How do you know that before your regular doctor says so?" I asked. Felicity colored faintly.

"Meredith, I appreciate the solicitude, but do remember I've had experience with pregnancy and miscarriages, and you haven't. I know I have to be careful, and I will be. I absolutely, definitely intend to have this baby. But if you don't want it born to a crazy lady, you'll have to protect me from too much hovering, not hover yourself! You got that?"

"Got it."

"Okay, then." Felicity smiled. "While we have this chance to talk alone, let's get something straight. You don't ever have to protect me from the truth. Not even hard truth. Because sometimes truth's all we have to hold to. On the other hand," she added, her eyes glinting, "you can protect me all you want from Fatma's rumors. They raise my blood pressure—from anger, not from fear."

"Okay, I got that too."

"Good." Felicity grinned. Then she hesitated, looking sheepish. "Having said all that, I have a favor to ask. When Mark calls—oh, he'll call," she added as I looked startled. "He always finds a way to somehow, when he's under cover. And when he does, I don't want him worried about my false alarms. In the situations he gets into, he needs his mind fully concentrated on what he's doing. For all our sakes."

I nodded slowly. Then the door opened, and Fatma came in carrying a tray, exactly as though the earlier scene had never taken place. She left without a word, without looking at me, and Felicity and I had a breakfast picnic on the bed.

During the morning I explored the house, with Matt and Rachel as my guides. It was not large, but it seemed spacious because of its three floors and many rooms, its galleries and its central court. Most of the rooms, with the exception of the main living room, were small, but they were high ceilinged, with hanging brass light fixtures like old lanterns. The ground-level rooms all opened onto the court, the upper ones onto the covered galleries. Some had walls all or partially tiled, and all had tile floors, often spread with Oriental rugs. The unusual proportions and furnishings made me feel out of place.

A small, formal sitting room was on one side of the front entrance corridor, and on the other side of it was Mark's study, a friendly, shabby room with a big work table and an old typewriter, a Byzantine icon, battered file cabinets and lots of bookshelves. Down the left side of the courtyard ran the kitchen and pantry and other work and store rooms where Kamil and Fatma presided ("Strictly off limits," Rachel warned me). Across the courtyard, oddly, was the dining room, facing the Farkas house. And across the whole back wall ran the living room. It was windowless, because it abutted the wall of the house on the street behind, but full of light because it opened on the court through many arches.

Above the fountain the court was open to the sky. "It rains in," Matt said with great delight. He dragged me up through a swift tour of the second floor (Mark and Felicity's room, two bathrooms, and some guest rooms), the third floor (kids' rooms; my room; bathroom; Fatma's room, off limits) and up to the flat rooftop.

There we stopped, and I gazed, speechless. The roof was a terrace, furnished with tables, chairs, and benches. A parapet just high enough to prevent the children from falling off the edge surrounded it. The house behind ours was farther down the hill, so though we looked down two stories to their rooftop they could not see us.

Rachel pointed out the Farkas house next door, separated from ours by a scant four feet of space. Their roof was grander, all flowering trees in ornate ceramic pots and furniture of elaborate wrought iron instead of wood. But the view from our rooftop could not be surpassed. Boats scurried back and forth on the water, and the domes of the Blue Mosque and of Santa Sophia glittered in the sun.

Rachel pointed. "That's Topkapi Palace, where Sultan Suleiman lived. We'll go there some day. There are the most gorgeous diamonds in the jewel rooms."

"And swords!" Matt said exuberantly. "A gold sword with an emerald *this big*." He twirled an imaginary scimitar enthusiastically above his head. Rachel was aghast.

"You know Mommy and Daddy don't like war games!"

"Huh!" Matt retorted, unperturbed. "You have to fight sometimes. Otherwise how can you make sure you'll never have to?" Irrefutable logic, but I wondered what his father thought of it. Matt saw my face and grinned. "Kamil's going to get me a scimitar," he confided. "To hang up on my wall. He said we'll get it the next time we go to the Covered Bazaar. You can help pick it out," he offered generously.

"You know we're not allowed to go to the Covered Bazaar." Rachel spoke that in typical older-sister tone, but there was a note underlying it that made me prick my ears. I glanced up to see a look pass between Matt and Rachel.

"Why not?" I asked sharply.

"Because Dad's afraid we'll get in trouble," Matt said with infinite scorn.

At that moment Rachel looked over the roof edge and saw Dr. Koc approaching our front door, so we all went in.

Moments later, Dr. el-Faisal, Felicity's obstetrician—a

brisk, gray-haired older woman—arrived. Both doctors went in to see Felicity, who was still in bed, and afterwards Dr. Koc found me in Mark's study.

"I'm concerned about your aunt," she said without preamble. "Are you prepared for the responsibility you've taken on?"

"She's not going to lose the baby, is she?" I gasped.

"There's no way of knowing. Her scare yesterday seems to have been harmless; but only time will tell. In the meantime she needs bed rest." Dr. Koc sat down in a carved wooden chair, her dark eyes grave. "Frankly, it would have been wiser for your aunt and uncle not to try for another child, but Felicity was determined. She means to be obedient, to look after herself, but—" Dr. Koc spread her hands. "Felicity is incapable of being detached from the life around her."

I nodded. "That's why Mark insisted that I come here."

"It would be more to the point if he were here, too," Dr. Koc said grimly. "Although perhaps, on second thought, that would be more dangerous." I stared at her, and she went on quickly, as if regretting her words. "You do understand that you must—how shall I put it?—be a dragon at Felicity's door. No news, nothing, no one must reach her that will upset her. You must be prepared to be an ogre when required."

"Like . . . when threats are made?"

For a minute there was no sound except the splashing of water in the courtyard fountain.

"My daughter talks too much," Dr. Koc said at last. "But it is just as well you know."

"You did hear about them, then?"

"Mark Greystoke told us. He and my husband are good friends, and Mark was . . . concerned about when Felicity returned. If he should not be here, you understand. He knew she must not be worried."

I took a deep breath. "Amina told me yesterday about the telephone calls, the ones when the line went dead. . . . Dr. Koc, you don't think Fatma's right—what she thinks, do you?" I could not bring myself to say the word *kidnapping*.

"It was to be expected your uncle would go underground just now," Dr. Koc said. *But she isn't answering my question,* my mind noted. "Whether he went on his own, or was sent, or sent for . . . the main thing is that your aunt and the children not be alarmed. Her obstetrician and I have agreed, Felicity must be made to stay in her room. That way it will be easier for you to shield her from—disturbance. And I think it would be wise for the television to be removed from the main room. Put it in your room, perhaps; that way you can monitor what the children see, and the servants cannot watch. I'll send one of our men over to help Kamil carry it up." Dr. Koc rose, her face softening. "Meredith, do not look so alarmed. All this is new and frightening, but I'm afraid in this part of the world it's just business as usual, as your uncle and aunt know too well. Now brighten your face, or you will scare Felicity! Oh, yes, Amina asked me to tell you she will telephone you later. She would like to have tea with you, or perhaps go sightseeing."

"Do you think I should?"

"Have I not just told you that you must carry on normally or Felicity will be suspicious?" Dr. Koc leaned forward and kissed me on both cheeks. "*Au revoir.* I will let you know when the television can be moved."

She left. Fatma served Felicity her lunch. The kids and I had lunch downstairs, in the dining room, ridiculously formal. "Fatma says we have to," Rachel said resignedly.

Twice during the meal the telephone rang, and each time Fatma answered. Each time she hung up soon, after some unintelligible but also unemotional conversation. So it hadn't been Amina. Or anonymous callers.

Or Brandon Hurd. The thought leaped into my mind out of nowhere, as I was helping myself to dessert of fresh figs and oranges after the second call. It startled me, and embarrassed me, to catch myself hoping for Brandon's call when there were much more serious matters to concern me.

Two o'clock came, and three. Rachel and Matt were playing up on the roof. Felicity was napping. Kamil went out somewhere. Fatma disappeared up to her room to rest. I went into Mark's study, picked out an illustrated guidebook to Istanbul, and curled up on the daybed with its pile of pillows. There was a telephone extension on Mark's work table, but it didn't ring. Amina didn't call. Brandon didn't call. Maybe he wasn't going to. I'd only known him for two days, after all. Maybe he'd only been going through the motions of being polite. He'd done so much for us already—

The telephone shrilled.

I leaped for it, forgetting I probably wouldn't be able to make myself understood. "Hello?"

"Hello? *Hello!* Who's there?" A man's voice startled me speechless. Then I gasped.

"Mark?"

"Who is that?"

"Mark, it's me, Meredith! Where are you?"

"Meredith—thank God. When I couldn't reach you at Delphi—" Mark's voice dropped and he spoke rapidly. "Don't speak, just listen. Quickly! Is Felicity there? Don't call her."

"She's in her room. Her doctor said she has to stay—"

"I understand. Tell her I called, that I'm fine. I'll phone when I can."

"Mark, listen! *Are* you all right? Really?"

I heard his familiar, reassuring laugh. "You know I lead a charmed life! Don't worry. Just do your job." He meant look after Felicity and the children. "Tell them I love them!"

There was a burst of sound in the background, then Mark's voice, muffled and indistinct as though he'd put his hand over the receiver. Then it was clear again, in a hurried whisper. *"Bismillahi ar rahman ar rahim.* Goodbye. God bless. Keep the faith!"

The line went dead.

When the knocks reverberated on the front door a few moments later, I almost screamed.

◇ 7 ◇

I put down the receiver and ran to the front door, my heart pounding. Then I discovered the peephole in the wooden door and looked through it, and my heart lurched back to normal.

Amina was standing outside, smiling.

I unlocked the door and threw it open, and she came in, her smile fading. "Something's wrong?"

"Nope, just me and my imagination." Something prompted me not to say anything about Mark's call. "Maybe I should say Fatma's imagination. I guess she's got me spooked."

"Spooked? That is American slang?"

"It means as if I'm feeling . . . ghosts, spirits."

"Ahh," Amina said knowingly. Her eyes softened. "That I understand. Mark says we Muslims are more attuned to such concepts than most Westerners."

Amina was a strange mixture of West and East herself, I thought. But I was suddenly very glad to have her there. I led the way across the court to the sitting room, and we curled up on the lemon-colored banquettes in a patch of sunlight.

"Your mom said you might come for tea. I'm glad you

did." I laughed. "That is, if you can tell me where the tea makings are! I don't know my way around the kitchen yet."

"And you'd better not try to learn! Ring for Fatma; she'll be mortally offended if you don't. You'll have dishonored her. Honor's very important to us Muslims, you know."

That was the second time she'd made a point of saying she was Muslim. I pulled the bellpull Amina pointed out, and when Fatma appeared I asked for tea. After Fatma'd gone off, grimly pleased, I looked at Amina.

"You're trying to tell me something about Muslims and Christians, aren't you? What? That the two don't mix?"

Amina looked at me with the same unwavering gaze her mother had, and Fatma, and Kamil. "Maybe that they— what did Mark say you call it?—*mix it up* too often. Because there is so much they don't understand about each other. Maybe I'm trying to warn you."

"So warn me," I said steadily. "Say what you want straight out, don't beat around the bush."

Amina spread her hands with a rueful laugh. "You see what I mean? You blurt things straight out. We speak around things, we tell truths in stories."

"So do Jews, only they call them parables. So do Christians, for that matter."

"Except the same symbols—they mean different things in the different cultures. Just like words do."

"You can say that again. And it's not just between religions. It's also between generations, or between people with different ideas in the same country." I was remembering again that Christmas Eve, and the conversation between Gramp and Mark. And this morning on the roof, Matt talking about weapons—

"What is it?" Amina asked instantly.

I shook my head. "Matt wants a scimitar. I think he has visions of defending us here while Mark's away. A man has to do what he has to do, and all that. Mark would be appalled."

"Mark Greystoke is a wonderful man. We all respect him very much. But he—" Amina bit her lip and shrugged.

"Go on," I said. "You think he's kind of crazy, is that it?"

"No, not crazy. Just—" Again, that Middle Eastern shrug. "He understands the Arab world better than any Westerner I know, but he still doesn't see why there is violence. He understands what the beliefs are that underlie it. The thousands of years of conflicts. The way some sects believe the United States—the West, Western ideas—are the Great Satan. The teaching that to die in a holy war is the best death, because the soul goes straight to Allah."

She spoke quietly, but there was an intensity beneath her words that shook me.

"I thought," I said deliberately, "that you Turks considered yourselves Europeans, and not Arabs."

"Now you are angry. I have offended you. I am sorry." Suddenly there were tears in Amina's eyes. But she still looked straight at me, not away, as I or people back home would have done. It was my eyes that fell.

" 'We Turks' do consider ourselves European," Amina said steadily. "Ever since Ataturk, our great liberator, pulled us into the modern world and this century. But only a tiny bit of Turkey is on the continent of Europe. True, ethnically the Turkish people are not Arab, but they are *Muslim.* Arab Muslims . . . there is a prejudice against non-Arabs. *I,*" she finished almost defiantly, "am half Arab. My mother is Turkish. My father is a Saudi. So I am—what is the English word for it?—a mongrel."

All at once the air in the long room was almost too close to breathe.

A shadow fell. Fatma, coming with our tray of tea. I wondered if she'd overheard. She set the brass tray on a stand in front of me, and said something in Turkish to Amina, who answered sharply.

Fatma left. Silence fell. I lifted the ornate teapot with hands that shook. "Shall I pour?" I asked, my voice cracking slightly.

"Please. With lemon and sugar, please." Amina, too, had been drilled in manners. "I am sorry," she said carefully, stirring her cup with a small silver spoon, "to have given you a lecture in our history."

"Don't be. It was fascinating. I know I have a lot to learn." I glanced at her, then away. "I guess I was—upset. About Matt and the scimitar and stuff." I didn't say, *about Mark, and the hostages,* but I knew she understood. "Matt sounded so much like my grandfather."

"Tell me about him," Amina said softly.

It was my turn to shrug. "How can you describe somebody who's part of your life? He's just always been there. For Mom, for Felicity, for me. When I was a kid he was always the one I could run to, to make things better. His great-grandfather was a pioneer who crossed the American prairie in a covered wagon and fought off Indian attacks. Gramp's an ex-marine, and he still believes in bullet diplomacy."

"Like one of your American movie heroes. Clint Eastwood, Sylvester Stallone. I see," Amina murmured. I thought she did. I was even more sure when she added unexpectedly, "Mark Greystoke . . . has your Aunt Felicity heard from him?"

"Didn't you know? Your mother's vetoed Felicity's having telephone conversations. And I haven't figured out how to cope with Turkish telephone operators yet." It wasn't exactly a lie, but my fingers shook slightly as I picked up one of Fatma's sticky pastries and bit into it. "This is good," I said around a mouthful of honey and crumbs.

Amina's eyes searched my face probingly, but she accepted the change of subject. "That's a Lady's Navel." She burst into laughter at my reaction. "All through this part of the world, pastries do have the most literal names." She pointed to the plate. " 'Ladies' navels,' 'firemen's hoses,' 'lips of the beauty.' Basically they're all *kurabiye,* deep-fried dough with sweet lemon syrup, but the shapes differ. And those phyllo things are *fararer,* 'bird's nests.' It's not just pastry that has names straight from the harem, either. We call our oval meatballs *kadin budu,* 'lady's thighs.' Speaking of the harem, I came to invite you for a tour of the Seraglio at Topkapi Palace. But perhaps it's too late to go today."

"I'm afraid it is." I really didn't want to go out. In case Brandon Hurd called. In case Mark called again. To my shame, I realized it had been Brandon I'd thought of first.

I glanced at my watch. Five-thirty. He wouldn't call now. Maybe he'd forgotten about calling at all.

"Another time, then. When things settle down. But tomorrow morning, before the heat comes, let's go out shopping. I'll show you around the modern city, where it's okay to go unchaperoned and so forth. Yes?"

The mention of chaperones startled me, and so did the trace of—what was it? a kind of loneliness?—in Amina's voice. I nodded.

"Tomorrow, then." Amina rose. Impulsively, she put her hand over mine. "*Salaam,* Meredith. I am sure you will hear from your uncle. Or whoever."

"What you said about being half-Arab," I said suddenly. "Does it give you any problems?"

Amina's eyes widened with a start. Then, as surely as if she'd drawn a veil across them, they showed nothing. "I? I am lucky, being in an international family. Living in Stamboul. We don't have wars here anymore. Or terrorists." Was it my imagination, or did her voice flatten slightly on that word? "My father's in international trade, he met my mother at the Sorbonne, so they're both very modern. I'm going to be a Golden Bracelet, like my mother."

And she went, with Fatma materializing like a ghost to show her out. I didn't have a chance to ask what that strange phrase meant. But I had suspicions, sharp and deep, that Amina was hiding something, and that she was afraid.

I knew it was ridiculous for me to sit around the house on the off-chance that Brandon Hurd would call. He hadn't called. He wasn't going to call, I told myself. He'd probably had enough of us, with all the help he'd given on our journey. He'd probably forgotten about asking to meet Mark. Mark wasn't here, anyway.

Then the phone rang, and all my proud defenses fled.

I plunged toward the extension in the entryway. "Hello? Greystoke residence." I remembered just in time to answer that way, not to give my name.

There was a silence, and then I thought I heard the sound of breathing. And then — nothing.

"Hello? *Hello?*" I shouted. Again, that silence. Not an empty silence; there was a faint hollow sound at intervals in the background. Then, just as I was about to ring for Fatma, there was a click. A dial tone came.

I stood there in the shaft of late afternoon sunlight coming from the courtyard, and I felt cold inside.

Something moved over the courtyard tiles. Fatma was coming, silent footed, to collect the tea tray. She stopped, staring. I held the dead receiver toward her. "The phone rang, but when I answered it, no one was there."

"It is servants' duty to answer telephone." She said

duty; what she meant was *right.* She took the receiver from my nerveless fingers and returned it to its cradle, and I let her do it.

Next time I'm getting to the phone faster, I thought. I wonder if there's a way to get a phone up in my bedroom. I wonder if there's a phone in Felicity's room!

I ran upstairs, and found Felicity just waking from a nap. "I feel like a sultan's favorite in the Seraglio, with all this time on my hands," she said, grinning. "Much as I hate admitting it, Suni Koc was right. I did get overtired. Telephone? Heavens no, there aren't any on the third floor! We had enough red tape getting one put in here, and Suni's taken that one away from me! What's the matter?" Felicity asked, eyes twinkling. "Are you afraid of missing a call from your new beau?"

I blushed. "I'm afraid my new beau's forgotten me. I was just thinking, in case Mark called again, during the night—" Too late, I remembered I hadn't told her about the earlier call, so I sat down on the edge of the bed and gave Felicity a carefully edited version.

"I guess I'll live without the sound of his voice for a few days. Or a few weeks," Felicity said philosophically. "This isn't the first time he's gone off to God alone knows where." She must have seen the doubt on my face, because she added, "Meredith, love, don't worry! Really! Mark leads a charmed life." There were those words again. "Besides," she added, "even when we can't speak, we communicate."

I knew it; that was what I feared.

"Is there any further information on the hostages?" Felicity asked suddenly.

I shook my head.

"Try to find out. Please. I want to know."

"I can't make head or tail of Turkish TV," I said with what I hoped sounded like normal aggrievement. "And no, Dr. Koc says you can't have that here, either!"

"Send Kamil out for a French- or English-language newspaper. Or—" Felicity swung her legs out of bed. "Where's my phone directory? I'll mark the names of some of our friends from the Society of Friends, or at Mark's office, that you can call for information."

I was saved from wriggling out of that one by the arrival of Fatma. "Madame go back to bed. I bring her dinner soon. Miss Meredith wanted on the telephone."

I heard Felicity insisting she'd have dinner on the table by the window as I ran downstairs.

Fatma had answered the extension in Mark's study, and I went there too, closing the door behind me. "This is Meredith Blake. Is Mark Greystoke there?" I actually did have Mark foremost on my mind, so much so that I was jolted when there was a pause and then a somewhat awkward laugh.

"Sorry to disappoint you. This is Brandon Hurd. I don't know if you remember. . . ." There was a note of uncertainty in his voice, and it thrilled and warmed me.

"Of course I remember," I said quickly. "How are you? How's your hotel?"

"Grim, I'd say. How is your aunt?"

"Not too good, I'm afraid."

"I'm sorry." There was sympathy in his voice, and disappointment too. "I was hoping I could take you out to dinner, but I suppose under the circumstances . . . Did you say your uncle isn't there?"

"No, he's not." There was a silence, as if Brandon understood I couldn't elaborate. I took a deep breath and said boldly, "It's too late to plan anything for tonight. Could I take a rain check? It will probably be okay for me to go out tomorrow."

"Great," Brandon said promptly. "How about I pick you up at seven? I'll call ahead to make sure we're still on, and you can leave a message for me here if you need to." He gave the number, and I wrote it down. "Tell your aunt I hope she's feeling better."

"I will. Brandon, have you heard any news about the men who were kidnapped?"

"Not much. I'll see if I can dig up anything more by tomorrow night. See you at seven then? Great."

He hung up, and I went upstairs to report to Felicity, now in a caftan beside the window, that I was obeying directions and not spending my time worrying.

"Good!" Felicity said firmly.

A sudden thought struck me. "Amina said something about chaperones. I don't need one, do I?" I asked apprehensively.

"Not unless you want to knock that nice young man for a loop! Americans are allowed more leeway than natives," Felicity said, "so long as they stick to respectable public places. Don't feel too sorry for Amina. Her parents are very modern. Mr. Farkas may expect her to be a bit more decorous because of his constantly doing business with conservative Moslems from other countries. But from what I've seen she doesn't suffer overmuch!"

She suggested that I round up the kids and tell Fatma the family would all have dinner up there together, so I obeyed. After dinner we played cards. Matt won; he was a regular card shark. "He cheats," Rachel said flatly, and Matt was indignant. They wrangled, bringing up all sorts of charges against each other till Felicity and I were weak with laughter. It was, all in all, a fun evening.

Two hours after we were all in bed, the telephone rang. Kamil was in bed and also slightly deaf, and Fatma was upstairs and apparently didn't hear. I was on the third floor, on the other side of the gallery, but I did hear, and I ran down the two flights barefoot as it rang and rang.

When I answered, there was no response. No vocal response, although somewhere at the other end of the line I could hear in the background the same hollow noise I'd heard before. Then there was a click, and the line went dead.

I didn't tell Felicity about it the next day.

Amina came for me shortly after nine a.m., and we walked farther uphill toward the main shopping district. The area was a disconcerting mixture of East and West— expensive modern jewelry stores next to hole-in-the-wall shops that sold belly-dance costumes and encouraged bargaining. Shop signs were in Turkish, French, and English. Music blared from many doorways, with a decidedly Eastern beat, minor-key and mysterious, but loud.

Amina laughed. "I told you Stamboul's a melting pot!"

We bought "gold" and "silver" filigree earrings, Amina pointing out the metal could be anything but that I could wear the drops from my good gold earwires for safety's sake. We looked at gorgeous pullovers and skirts and dresses in vivid shades, adorned with embroidery and crocheted lace. At least I looked; Amina shook her head.

"Hold off till I take you to the Covered Bazaar for those. You can haggle there and get much better prices."

"You sound like a regular bedouin trader," I accused her, laughing.

Amina shrugged. "Perhaps I am," she said, and I remembered her comment about being a mongrel and half-Arab.

We went on up one side of the street and down the other. The heat was building as the sun rose higher, and I was starting to feel claustrophobic. People pushed right in to us; if I stopped at a window, they kept right on charging toward me. I was conscious of hot puffs of breath, garlicky or lemony, and of eyes staring at me.

All at once it seemed as if the world was full of eyes, all dark, all focused on me with a measuring insolence.

Amina grasped my arm. "Come on," she said. "You've had enough." She steered me into a small cafe. It was modern and air conditioned. We sat down at a tiny table, and Amina ordered coffee and more of those fascinating pastries.

I hated Turkish coffee but couldn't say so. I sipped it slowly and concentrated on the cakes. They were rich and sticky sweet.

"Don't eat them if you don't want to," Amina said. "You don't have to drink the coffee, either. I had to order something so we could sit down." She asked the waiter for a soft drink, and when it came I swallowed gratefully.

"Are you all right now?" Amina asked at last. I nodded.

"Good. For a minute I was afraid you would pass out."

"Oh, come on!" I said indignantly, with totally false assurance.

Amina ignored that. "You aren't used to our heat. Or the crowding." I glanced at her, startled, and she nodded her head slightly in understanding. "Mr. Greystoke has told me," she said, "about spatial differences in different cultures. Scientific studies have been done about it. You are used to more private space, yes? On the outside of your bodies, and in your rooms?"

"You wouldn't say that if you saw New York City," I said.

"I don't mean that. I have seen you Americans in movie theaters," Amina said amusedly. "When you sit down, you always leave a pair of seats between you and your nearest neighbors. We do not. Our . . . selves . . . start way deep down inside us. The space on the outside is public space. Anybody can take it just by moving in. And families—they do not need separate rooms like you do, or such large ones. What we need is the sky. Or the feeling of it. I've seen American houses in movies, all those rooms but such low ceilings, and no sky." She grimaced, her eyes mischievous.

"At least we don't have chaperones," I pointed out.

"And maybe you find sometimes they'd come in handy?" Amina answered with equal innocence. She ordered another soft drink and started on her third pastry. "Forgive me, I do not know you long, but may I say something? You do not know customs here. I think maybe even Mr. and Mrs. Greystoke do not know dating customs here. Maybe, if a young man asks to take you out, a chaperone would be wise."

"Not if it's an American young man," I said. Amina's eyes widened, and I ended up telling her all about Brandon Hurd. "The only thing is," I concluded, "he's all for logic, and I tend to act first and think later."

"Hmm," Amina said. "I knew you, too, saw with the third eye. It's a Sufi phrase," she explained quickly when I blinked. "Sufism is Muslim mysticism. To see with the third eye means you . . . know with the soul, with intuition, not just with logic or experience."

"You just hit the nail on the head," I said ruefully. "My third eye sees the possibility of big fights coming. What about you? Are you dating anyone? With or without chaperones?"

Amina dropped her eyes. It was the first time I'd seen her do that. "There is a young man. His name is Ali. He is the brother of a school friend, and we see each other at the library, or at the mosque. Outside the mosque—inside, men and women do not sit together."

"You don't date?" I asked incredulously. Amina shook her head and changed the subject, and that was the last I was able to get out of her about Ali. When we left the cafe, Amina hailed a cab to drive us home.

I found Felicity still dutifully upstairs but ordering Fatma, Kamil, and two tall, tanned Western men I didn't recognize around. They were busily transforming the guest room next to the master bedroom into a sitting room, under the supervision of Felicity and a pleasant-faced, middle-aged Englishwoman.

"I may have to stay upstairs, but I don't have to stay in a bedroom," Felicity said firmly. "Meredith, this is Edith Hibborn, from the Society of Friends. And Tom Truscott and Will Sheldon, also from our Meeting. Tom, if you drag that bedstead down to the courtyard Kamil will stick it somewhere. Then bring up the little sofa from the front parlor. Otherwise I think everything can stay where it is. Oh, except for the television. I'd like that up here."

"No way," I said loudly. "Dr. Koc has already said no." I appealed mutely to Mrs. Hibborn, and she agreed promptly.

"My husband always says the main purpose TV serves anyway is to raise our blood pressure! You know Mark will see you know everything you need to, and probably a lot more. I'll loan you a stereo, if you'd like one."

"Thanks, we have a good one. Meredith, maybe you can bring some records up here later." Felicity looked as if she were getting tired.

"Right. Well done, everyone," Mrs. Hibborn said briskly. "Tom, Will, let's clear out and leave these good people in peace. I'll call you later to see if there's more we can do to help." It was me she said that to, not Felicity. I went down to the front door with them to see them out.

I had lunch with Felicity in the new sitting room. "We had two mysterious phone calls before Edith Hibborn got here and started the redecorating project," she told me. "Don't worry, I didn't go downstairs. I had the door to my room open, and I could tell what the calls were by the way Fatma was shouting. She always curses in Turkish when there's a wrong number, and when it's a dead line she starts shouting about kidnapping." Felicity burst out laughing. "I keep telling you, calls like that, and rumors, are an occupational hazard in our kind of life! You either take them with a grain of salt or you go mad. Stop looking like that and tell me about your morning. How many pairs of earrings did Amina talk you into buying, how much did she pry out of you about your Greek god, and what time is he coming by tonight?"

I turned red. "Two. Not much. At seven. Anything else you want to know?" I asked. Felicity grinned. "Okay, then, you tell me," I went on. "What do you know about this mysterious boyfriend of Amina's?"

"Not as much as I'd like to," Felicity said frankly. "So she did talk to you about him. I hoped she would."

"Why?"

"Because Suni Koc's having kittens about him, and I'm not sure why. Suni's usually very progressive. And it's not as if she has cause to worry for the usual reason. From what she says this boy's so religious he's a regular prude."

"Muslim?"

"Of course, or both Suni and Mustapha would really be having fits. I can't make out whether it's because Amina's too young and they're getting too serious, or whether they really don't know why they're bothered."

"Sounds like the way Dad is over me sometimes."

"Not to mention the way your grandfather was over your mother and me. Still is." She stretched out on the sofa and reached for a magazine. "Have fun tonight! Come in and give us a fashion parade before you leave; Rachel will love that. And bring Brandon in to say hello when you get back, if it's not too late."

Brandon called that afternoon to confirm our date.

"I've made a reservation at the Sheraton's roof restaurant," he said. That called for a special effort, and I made it, with a sheer sleeveless dress of changeable brown-and-gold organza and the new gold-colored harem earrings. And my hair French-braided down the back. And high-heeled sandals. When I was dressed I went in to show Felicity and the kids, as I had promised, and they were suitably impressed.

"Our dinner isn't ready yet, so you can bring Brandon up when he comes, if you'd like to," Felicity suggested.

"Maybe later," I said vaguely. I had a clear memory of Matt's talent for embarrassing remarks and questions. Not on a first date, I decided, and laughed aloud. All at once it felt so good, so *normal*, to be waiting for a date. A dinner date at a big hotel with a gorgeous guy four years older than I—some *normal*, I thought, and grinned.

I went downstairs to wait, with Felicity thoughtfully keeping the kids upstairs. As I put my foot on the bottom step, I heard a muffled sound of voices. Not live voices—I traced the sound to the sitting room, and found Fatma and Kamil standing gazing at the TV screen.

On the screen, Mark Greystoke, in desert shirt and pants, was walking with a number of armed men in Arab headgear. Their weapons glistened in the sun. Mark looked so calm, so ordinary. The TV commentator was rattling on in excited Turkish.

"What is he saying?" I demanded sharply.

Fatma turned to me with that favorite expression of grim triumph and said something in Turkish. Then she translated. "The League of the Sons of the Prophet. They have claimed credit for kidnap of the infidel devils."

League of the Sons of the Prophet . . . that's one we haven't heard of, I thought numbly. Then another, more terrible thought struck. "You don't mean—they aren't holding *Mark*—"

Kamil cut in, with a spate of sharp Turkish that kept Fatma silent. Then he turned to me, with labored, careful English. "Mr. Greystoke, he is well. He go as friend. He try to help. He has friends—both sides."

"Yes, I understand that. Thank you, Kamil." I snapped off the TV and turned to Fatma. "Mrs. Greystoke must hear *nothing* of this. Will you help me keep it from her?" They got the point; they nodded solemnly. "Good," I said as the doorbell rang. I went to the door and met Brandon.

"Greystoke was on TV, did you see?" he asked at once. I nodded. "I've nosed around," Brandon said as he led me to the waiting taxi. "I haven't heard much. There's the usual stuff, background of the hostages and of your uncle, in the European papers. We can get copies for you at the newsstand in the Sheraton. This Sons of the Prophet group is something new, isn't it? Nobody seems to have heard of them before."

"I know I haven't."

"New groups start every week or so, from what I hear.

Especially among the young guys. Looking for honor, or spiritual brownie points, or something." He helped me into the cab, and from then on we didn't talk about the hostage situation. Partly that was wariness of being overheard, in spite of the unlikelihood of the taxi driver understanding. Partly—okay, mostly on my part at least— it was a wanting to preserve the magic. Because the night *was* magic.

The restaurant was on the roof, and the view through the yards of plate glass was all splendor. The Golden Horn, and the Galata Bridge gleaming in the late rays of the sun. The mosque dome and minaret spires, also gleaming. I pointed to them. "They're like the gold in the jewelry stores. I've never seen such yellow gold before," I said bemusedly. "I can't believe it."

"Like your eyes," Brandon teased. "The Greeks called those with gold eyes 'the Children of the Sun.' They're supposed to have special gifts, as I recall. Medea was the most famous of them."

"I don't think I particularly want to take after Medea. Isn't she the one who killed her brother and cut him up in little pieces to keep her father from chasing after her and Jason of the Golden Fleece when they eloped? And killed her own children later?"

"Sure, after Jason dumped her for a Greek wife who just happened to be the king's daughter and half Medea's age. Talk about dirty politics," Brandon retorted, laughing. "I believe he also said something about Medea being a dirty heathen who ought to be properly grateful for being brought to Greece to be civilized."

"Then I don't blame her for wanting to get even."

"Such bloody vindictiveness from a certified pacifist?" Brandon looked at me in mock horror. "Seriously, though, Jason and Medea were a classic case of cultural conflict. Each wanted to be valued by the standards of his or her own culture, yet judged the other by that same standard, without making allowances for difference of beliefs or meanings."

My eyes met his. "The way some cultures think that violence is the only way left to get what they want," I said. "And other cultures—ours—don't know enough about them to try to find other solutions." He nodded, and I know we were both thinking of Mark.

After that, Mark was like an invisible third party at our table. But I still found myself growing closer to Brandon as we ate, made light tourist talk, and danced.

"Want to leave?" Brandon asked at last, after we had watched the lights of the Golden Horn and the Galata Bridge twinkle against a black-velvet sky as we sipped coffee—real American coffee. I nodded. The headwaiter brought me a long-stemmed pink rose to take with me.

We went from the dining room into the restaurant's outer lobby. A large-screen television was turned on, with several people grouped around it. Brandon glanced at it, and put his hand beneath my elbow. "Come on, we can just catch that elevator."

"No wait." I glanced, too, and then stopped dead. "Please! I want to see."

One of the international news channels was broadcasting. A man I vaguely recognized as an American bureaucrat was speaking. I certainly recognized the American flag behind him, and the Great Seal of the United States on the lectern. Instinctively I moved closer, and Brandon followed.

The TV set showed English-language captions. The League of the Sons of the Prophet had charged Stephen Althorp and the American journalist of being spies for the CIA, and were holding them in "some secret place, probably Lebanon or Iran" before bringing them up before a Muslim court of justice.

And both the League of the Sons of the Prophet and the U.S. Government were disavowing Mark Greystoke's unauthorized efforts to act as a mediator.

·10·

I could feel all the blood running from my face. I turned to Brandon blindly. "I've got to get home! If the TV's on there—" I had no faith in Fatma's promise—or for that matter, in Felicity's staying upstairs.

"I hear you," Brandon said quietly. He hurried me to the elevator, which blessedly came quickly. He tipped the hotel doorman lavishly, and the doorman hustled up a taxi. We reached the house.

"*Darn,* I forgot to ask Felicity for a key!" We'd have to ring the doorbell, and that meant encountering Fatma or Kamil. I prayed it would be Kamil, or that at least Fatma had not been watching the TV.

Brandon rang the bell. I waited, shifting my weight from one foot to the other. "Calm down," Brandon said.

"Why doesn't anybody *come?*"

"Probably the old lady's in bed." I'd told Brandon about Fatma over dinner. "Or it takes her a while to get here—no, someone's coming."

We could hear somebody fumbling with the lock on the inside. The door opened, and Rachel stood there, looking pale beneath her tan in her long white nightgown. And far behind her, running through the sitting room arch, was

Matt. Matt, calling in a stage whisper, "Mer, come quick! Daddy's on TV!"

I could hear Brandon shutting and locking the front door behind us as I ran to Matt.

The television set was on, its sound turned low, and I dropped down on my knees before it just as Matt and Rachel did. Mark was no longer on camera, but the screen showed Islamic fundamentalist militants shouting with clenched, raised fists.

"How much Turkish or Arabic do you guys know?" I asked with apprehension.

"A little," Rachel said. "Those men are in Lebanon. They say Mr. Althorp and Daddy and that journalist are 'American imperialist spies.' "

"That's crazy," Matt said loudly.

"Matt!" Rachel warned. The picture changed to another news story, and she reached out to snap the television off.

"What are you two doing down here?" I demanded. "Where's Fatma? Where's your mother?"

Rachel and Matt exchanged glances. "Mommy's in bed," Rachel said in a low voice. "So's Fatma. Kamil was supposed to get up and let you in when you got home. He sleeps off the kitchen." She jerked her head in that direction. "But he's kind of deaf, he doesn't always hear."

"So you guys decided you'd take advantage of that and sneak down and watch TV?"

"We do sometimes. When it's hot and we can't sleep. Fatma has ten fits if she catches us, and Mom's not thrilled. But Daddy—" Rachel gulped. "Daddy just chases us to bed and tells us not to upset Mommy. He thinks it's funny. Depending on what we're watching . . ."

"And tonight you got more than you bargained for," I finished softly. Rachel nodded.

"It's crazy, that American spy stuff," Matt repeated. "Mr. Althorp's British." But there was a look of uncertainty in his eyes. Suddenly, miserably, he butted his head against my shoulder. I hugged him hard and reached my other arm around Rachel.

"You're right, it's crazy," I said staunchly. "You know your dad works for a religious group, not the government. And anyway, the big thing about your dad is that he won't take sides."

"The big thing about Daddy is that everybody likes him," Rachel said stoically. "Everybody talks to him. That's why he's so good at—" She didn't finish.

"Right. And why we're not going to let ourselves get spooked." I made my voice as brisk and level as I could. "Speaking of which, we'd better not say anything about those rumors we just heard. To anybody."

"'Course not. We know that." Matt got up and turned to Brandon, who'd so far been ignored. "You Mer's new boyfriend? I'm Matthew Greystoke."

"I'm Brandon Hurd." Brandon shook hands formally with Matt, with Rachel. Matt started for the stairs.

"Coming, Rache?" he said with authority, and Rachel followed.

Brandon stood behind me, his hand on my shoulder, and we watched them mount the two flights of stairs, their shadows stretching eerily along the tile walls. I turned to Brandon, my eyes full of tears.

"I know," Brandon said. "I know." He handed me a

handkerchief, and I wiped my eyes. Brandon glanced at the TV set. "Is it a good idea for that to stay here?"

"No, it's not. It's supposed to be taken up to my room. Why didn't I make sure it was locked there before I left?"

Brandon calmly strode over and unplugged the set. "No time like the present," he said. He carried it upstairs with me guiding him. We stopped at the second level while I checked Felicity. She was sleeping.

"It's all right. She didn't hear," I whispered. We went up the next flight as soundlessly as possible, past Rachel and Matt's closed doors. Brandon set the TV down on the table in my room and wiped his forehead.

"I don't know how to thank you. For everything."

"No problem," Brandon said gently. We went back down, and at the door he paused. "May I call you tomorrow?"

"I wish you would. And if you hear anything—"

"Don't worry, I will." He looked at me and then leaned forward and kissed me. And let himself out while I still stood there, overcome and silent.

The taxi had long since left, but I could hear Brandon's footsteps receding up the street. At last I stirred, locked the door, and went back into the sitting room to return the pillows, evidence of the kids' nighttime TV watching, from the floor to the banquette.

And the phone rang.

For a second, literally, I was paralyzed. Late night phone calls always did that to me, because in our house they only meant emergencies. Or what my mother called "creepy callers." I pried my feet loose from the sitting room floor, and flew across the courtyard. *Creepy callers* was exactly what this was. The same awareness of someone's breathing, more sensed than heard; the same hollow, rhythmic sounds in the background. I jammed the phone back on the receiver and stood there, shaking.

The phone rang again.

I would have just unplugged it, except there was the other phone in the study, and it, too, was ringing. Felicity might have heard the phone from upstairs.

I forced myself to pick it up and said *"Yes?"* harshly.

My mother's voice, shocked and alarmed, said, *"Meredith?"*

"Mom? . . . Oh, *Mom—"*

"Yes, it's Mother. Baby, what is it? Are you all right?"

"Yes. I'm just startled—it's the middle of the night here."

"Oh, Lord, I forgot that." My mother sounded relieved, but not very much. "When I couldn't reach you in Greece—you were supposed to still be there. . . . Meredith, is Felicity all right? Has anything happened?"

I made myself breathe slowly so my voice would sound calm. "Felicity's fine. She had a false alarm, and her doctor's making her stay in bed for now, but she's fine. We came back early because a friend of Mark's was taken hostage. Mom, if you're calling because of the charges of CIA connections, I already know about that. *I* do; she doesn't."

Mother interrupted. "A special news bulletin just cut in on my soap opera. Mark went on camera somewhere in Lebanon, with a bunch of Shiite militants."

"Oh, Mom, no!"

"Oh, yes. Are you really surprised?" Mother asked

grimly. "Darling, Mark announced that he's made contact with this Sons of the Prophet group through intermediaries, and they're taking him to see Stephen Althorp and that journalist. He hopes to see some of the earlier hostages, too. He thinks he's going to be able to negotiate their release."

"Negotiate—"

"*Not* with the blessings of the secretary of state or Congress," Mother said. "He's gone alone, of course. Unarmed. I thought you'd better know in case the press starts showing up on your doorstep."

"Dear God," I said slowly.

"I know, darling. But at least this means they're still alive," Mother said optimistically. "Meredith, if you need me or Daddy, if Felicity needs us, call. I'll come, we'll both come. So would Gran and Gramps."

"The last thing we need here," I said, "is Gramps and the marines."

I slept, but fitfully. Early in the morning I went downstairs to find the kids eating breakfast quietly, not betraying by the flicker of an eye what had occurred last night. If they questioned the removal of the TV, they didn't do it where I could hear. Fatma said nothing about Mark, so I presumed she hadn't heard. I accompanied her up with Felicity's breakfast, just in case. Felicity was full of suggestions that I, too, take the bedroom next to mine and turn it into a private sitting room. That might not be a bad idea, I decided, thinking of both the TV set and Brandon Hurd.

Immediately after breakfast, Dr. Koc arrived. She'd

seen the TV news and wanted to make sure Felicity hadn't. I brought her up to date.

"I'm glad you got the TV upstairs." Dr. Koc shook her head. "It's *most* unfortunate the children saw. My fault, for not making sure the set got moved yesterday. I did send a boy over in the early evening, but he needed Kamil's help and couldn't find him."

"Rachel told me Kamil doesn't always hear when he's called. He's pretty old." I was remembering Kamil's leathery face and missing teeth. "Anyway," I added, "the kids promised not to say anything to their mother. They were pretty strong about the whole thing."

"They've had to be, poor little things." Dr. Koc rose. "All the same, make sure the door to the room the TV's in is locked, and you keep the key. I should keep the door to your bedroom locked as well. It's unpleasant to say, but standards of privacy here are not what you're used to. The servants have been with this house a long time, and they take liberties."

I felt uncomfortable. Dr. Koc smiled. "You're going through culture shock. Don't be embarrassed. Now let us plan an amusement for Felicity, who is getting very bored. She is feeling so much better today that I would like to have you and her come to my home for dinner. I will send manservants over to carry her downstairs and push her next door in a wheelchair. Fatma will give the children their dinner here. What do you say?"

I thanked her and accepted, repressing the disloyal thought that now I couldn't see Brandon again this evening.

Fatma appeared to let Dr. Koc out the front door, and when the doctor had gone she turned to me. "If I may speak with you, Miss?"

"Yes—of course." I followed the old woman into Mark's office, where she shut the door and leaned against it, her arms folded. "Is something wrong?"

"It is right I should tell you since the Madame is sick. Kamil is gone."

I looked at her blankly. "What do you mean, gone?"

"He was not in his room this morning. He should have been in the kitchen at six to see to the stove and go to market. I went to his room, and he was not there. His bed did not look slept in."

Just as he had not been around to let me in last night. . . . I didn't say that. I said, "Thank you, Fatma. I'll look into it. By the way, Madame Greystoke and I will have dinner at the Farkas home tonight. Will you see to the children's dinner and get them to bed?"

"Yes, Miss." Fatma didn't say *of course*, but I could see it in her eyes.

I went through the house from top to bottom. There was no sign of Kamil until I reached the roof and saw him watering the plants in the courtyard far below. I ran down and questioned him, and he looked at me blankly.

"No, Miss. Kamil here. All night. All morning."

"Then why couldn't Fatma find you?"

"Kamil at market." He turned away and began sweeping the courtyard's tiled floor vigorously.

The day passed. I told Felicity of Dr. Koc's dinner plans and Felicity was delighted. "It will be lovely to go visiting, and Suni serves fabulous meals." She stopped. "What if Mark should call while we're out?"

"Then Fatma will tell him where you are, and he can call you there! I'll take care of it." Inwardly I was wondering what explanation to come up with if Mark did not call soon. I'd heard too much about war-ravaged Lebanon. Were there working telephones in the secret Shiite safe house? More to the point, would Mark be allowed to use them?

In the late afternoon Brandon called to ask if he could come over after dinner. I explained why he couldn't. "Tomorrow, then," Brandon said. "Why don't I come in the morning? Maybe we could take the kids out somewhere for a while."

"That sounds great." I rang off with real regret.

But going to the Farkas house for dinner was a thrill. We dressed up, Felicity in a long embroidered Turkish dress ("Ideal maternity wear," she said) and I in a dark red dress I'd bought in Greece, and the harem earrings. The two manservants appeared as promised to carry Felicity downstairs and roll her off in a wheelchair. Rachel and Matt waved to us from the rooftop with Fatma behind them, scowling with disapproval. Fatma had become very protective of Felicity and the baby.

Our short trip along the sidewalk to the next house resembled a grand progress, with Kamil running ahead to ring the doorbell. We were watched by passengers in passing cars and loiterers on the sidewalk, whom Kamil shooed away.

Then we went into the Farkas house. I had gathered

from things Felicity had said that they were rich, but I hadn't been prepared for this.

To start with, the house was twice the size of ours. They had a walled garden behind the house, going downhill in terraces planted with flowers and cypress trees. On the far side of the house, also protected by walls, grew nut and fruit trees. The chandeliers were French and Russian, old bronze and crystal, and the floors were covered with Oriental rugs, old and magnificent. But the furniture, and the glowing paintings on the walls, were stark and modern.

Dr. Koc looked pretty magnificent herself, in a high-fashion black silk dress and heavy bright-gold jewelry set with emeralds. Amina's father wore a dinner jacket with the tiny red ribbon of the French Legion of Honor in his buttonhole. He was portly, brisk, and welcoming, with black eyes and silver-shot black hair and pointed beard.

"Felicity, my dear, how good to have you back! I hope we'll all dine together again soon, with Mark here as well. He is doing fine work, fine! He makes us proud to be his neighbors. And this is the niece from America? Welcome to Stamboul, Miss Meredith. I am glad you and my daughter have become already such very good friends."

"Don't monopolize her, Papa! I want to show Meredith the garden." Amina tucked her arm through mine and led me off. She was wearing even more black eyeliner than usual, and bright lipstick. But her face looked strained.

"Bring Meredith back in quickly, dear. Dinner's almost ready," Dr. Koc warned. So we only made a quick circuit around the fountain, with a gold-toothed gardener at our elbow, eagerly pointing out the finest specimens.

We dined, and I do mean dined. The meal began with

mezzes, or hors d'oeuvres—*humus*, a chick-pea and sesame-paste dip served with pita bread; little phyllo pastries called *sigara boreji; kofte*, small meatballs of ground lamb. It went on through *dogun corbasi*, the "wedding soup" reserved for special occasions (because, I learned later, it took so much time to make), to kabobs, both meat and fish, served on brass-handled skewers on a bed of pilaf.

We were on the Circassian chicken with yogurt-and-walnut sauce when Mr. Farkas turned to Felicity with a smile. "So do tell us, what have you heard from my good friend your husband?"

"Nothing for a day or so. He's very busy, you know," Felicity said, too brightly.

"Meredith, try some of this *tabbouleh* salad. It's one of our cook's specialties," Amina said loudly.

Dr. Koc was shooting daggers at her husband over Felicity's head. Mr. Farkas recovered quickly. "He'll be back in no time with more of his splendid stories, never fear. Meredith! How did you enjoy the art exhibition at the university last night? Amina was so pleased to take you to it, but I'm afraid she was very naughty keeping you out so late." His eyes twinkled behind his rimless glasses. "My daughter should have known better. Just because the coffeehouses remain open till that hour does not mean it's too wise for young girls to be at them after midnight— even though you were, as she says, 'quite safe with a group of students.'"

"But I wasn't—" I exclaimed involuntarily. And stopped abruptly as I saw the panic in Amina's eyes.

"I wasn't tired," I finished quickly.

"Meredith and I are still all out of sync with jet lag," Felicity put in, overlapping. "Mustapha, you still haven't told us, when did you get back from the buying trip? Where was it this time, China? What did you find?"

"Some excellent rugs and embroideries, in more contemporary colorways. The People's Republic is really working at becoming modern. Seduced by the lure of capitalism, perhaps!" Mr. Farkas chuckled. The moment passed; the conversation turned, steered deftly by Dr. Koc.

Dinner wound up in a flurry of fruits and pastries. We transferred into the library—brass-rimmed glass shelves of books and statuary, a vibrant crimson rug, cream- and silver-colored silk upholstery—for coffee.

Amina appropriated her cup and mine. "Mama, Papa— I would like to take Meredith to my room. I want to show her the courses I will be studying at the university in the fall. Will you excuse us?"

She was out the door, with me behind her, before the formalities were completed.

"Meredith, I am so sorry," Amina exclaimed as soon as we were upstairs in her room with the door shut and locked. "I hope Papa didn't upset your aunt. He just came home yesterday afternoon, and Mama was at the clinic then and in her office almost all today, she hadn't told him not to mention Mr. Greystoke—"

"Forget that," I said swiftly. "What was all that about you taking me to the university with you last night?"

Suddenly, abruptly, she sat down on the satin bedspread and put her hands up to her face.

"I am so sorry," she whispered. Tears sprang to her eyes, rolling in black tracks of eyeliner down her pale face, and she let them come.

"This is about your boyfriend, isn't it?" I said gently.

Amina nodded. "I didn't have a chance to tell you, but I tried. I did try, Meredith—when you came."

"That trip into the garden. Okay, I got that. But *what* were you trying to tell me?"

Amina spread her hands. "I had to see Ali—something had happened since the last time I saw him. I can't explain. I called his sister, and he sent word back through his sister where I should meet him. I knew Mama had clinic duty last evening, and I— Meredith, you do see, don't you? I had to talk with Ali before Papa came home, he wasn't due for another day or so, only then yesterday afternoon I heard he was coming last night. The only thing I could think of was to say I was showing you around, there really *is* an exhibition at the university, I thought I could take you there tomorrow so it wouldn't be a lie, not really. . . ."

"That's okay," I said. "It's over; let's just drop it. I don't think your father caught on. Your mother, I'm not sure."

"Mama's not quite so bad," Amina said optimistically. She went to the mirror and wiped her eyes. "That's because she's a Golden Bracelet, I guess. I'm very lucky."

"Golden Bracelet. You said that before. What does it mean?"

"That she's a career woman—modern. She even kept her maiden name after marriage. In the Middle East," Amina said, carefully relining her eyes, "there have always been wars. People have always been nomads, traders. People put their money in things easily portable, easily sold. Gems. Gold. Jewelry. A woman's dowry, her wealth, was always in gold jewelry she could wear. If her husband was killed, or if her husband said 'I divorce you' three times and cast her out, she had her jewelry so she could survive. But today's Turkish women can support themselves if need be, without selling anything. Their talent is their wealth. They are their own Golden Bracelets."

"And you said that's what you're going to be." She nodded. "How does Ali fit into that?" I asked carefully. "From what you said"—I tried hard to not blurt out anything Felicity had told me—"he sounded kind of conservative."

"Oh, he's all for my having a career. So long as it doesn't keep me too much away from him!" Amina giggled. "In some ways, he's very radical. Is that the right word? Just as in other ways, he has very strict ideas. Some people would call *them* radical, I guess. Papa can't stand Ali, but it's not Ali's fault he hasn't had all Papa's advantages! Though Papa's right, Ali *is* jealous." She surveyed her face very carefully, and laughed again. "Papa says Ali would like to see me wear a veil, but he's wrong. Definitely, Ali likes looking at me."

I followed Amina down to join our elders, feeling decidedly uneasy.

Nothing happened at our own house while we were out. No phone calls of any kind, and Kamil was on the premises all evening. I knew, because I asked Fatma in the morning. In the morning, too, Brandon came as promised. I let him in. We stood in the entry for a minute, smiling at each other.

"It's a gorgeous day out," Brandon said. "Why don't we take the kids somewhere? It will do them good. How about visiting the Grand Bazaar?"

"That has to wait a week or so. Felicity's birthday's coming up, and the bazaar's the best place they can buy gifts for her at a bargain."

"So why can't they buy gifts today?"

"Because Matt's already spent his next two weeks' allowance, that's why." We both laughed. "There's a swimming pool at the university. Mark gives some lectures there, so the Greystokes have pool privileges. Felicity suggested I take the kids there today."

So that's what we did. Afterward, I phoned Fatma not to expect us for lunch, and we bought kebabs at a pushcart and checked out the art exhibit, just in case Mr. Farkas asked me anything about it. I was afraid the kids would be bored, but Rachel liked it, and some paintings were so modern that Matt thought them absolutely hilarious.

"Let's walk home and get ice cream on the way," Brandon suggested, when Matt's reactions became too noisy. We bought the ice cream, and we kept on walking.

"Didn't anybody warn you Stamboul's a city of hills?" Brandon asked, eyeing my flimsy sandals.

"I knew that. I just didn't know there would be so many rocks to wear out cheap shoes!" I rubbed one aching arch over the other instep. We were out of the university district by now, in an area where the streets were rough.

The sun was hot, and even Rachel was getting cranky. Brandon steered us toward an open square. "It's a couple of miles farther, I'm afraid. Maybe we can get a taxi. It looks like there's a neighborhood market up ahead."

There was a market, but there were no taxis. Stalls were set on sidewalks, and there were battered pushcarts in the streets. In the square, umbrellas and makeshift tents had been erected. All of the vendors and most of the shoppers were men. I told myself the crowding and the unblinking stares were nothing personal, just part of the cultural difference everyone had pointed out. But I still wished I hadn't dressed the way I would for a hot day at home.

"I'm tired," Matt said abruptly in a small-boy voice.

Brandon and I exchanged glances. "Maybe we should stop for some soda pop or something," I said.

"Might not be a good idea," Brandon answered. "You can't always be sure bottled sodas haven't been opened and refilled with some local drink. How about oranges? I've got a knife; we can cut them open and suck the juice." I nodded, and he steered me into an open area where some elderly women were inspecting cooking pots with critical eyes. "Wait here. I'll be right back."

He loped off. I stood, holding onto Matt and Rachel tightly in the crowd. Rachel was subdued; Matt sat down in the street with elaborate patience.

I could feel walls of eyes looking at us. I looked off across space, avoiding eye contact, seeing Brandon's tall figure at the orange vendor's across the square. I felt acutely conscious of my pale skin showing through my summery clothes. First thing tomorrow I'm buying some dark sunglasses, I vowed. Then no one will be able to see into my eyes.

I heard, rather than saw, a ruckus break out close behind us.

Then someone jostled me, and at the same moment I felt Rachel squeeze my hand. I swung around. At a nearby pushcart, three men were fighting. One of them I'd never seen before. One was young, vaguely familiar—I squinted and then caught my breath. It was the servant with the gold tooth from the Farkas home. And the other—could it be Kamil?

Rachel jerked my hand, hard. I stared at her, and she stared straight back at me, imploring—no, *commanding* silence. I obeyed.

"Here we are." Brandon was back, his hands full of oranges. "Matt, if you'll dig in my right pants pocket, you'll find a knife."

It was a Swiss army knife, and Matt was enthralled. Matt cut the oranges carefully, under Brandon's supervision, and handed them around. When I turned, very casually, back in the direction of the pushcart, all three men were gone.

We walked the rest of the way home slowly, sucking

oranges. Fatma met us at the door, ignoring Brandon. "Miss Farkas, she waiting for you in the sitting room. She been here an hour."

"I know my cue," Brandon said. "Talk to you tomorrow." He went. Fatma led the children off, muttering complaints about their dust and sunburn. I walked across the courtyard, and Amina jumped up from the lemon-colored banquette.

"Meredith . . . thanks be." *She* was wearing dark glasses, even in the house. "I have to talk to you. Upstairs. Please."

I led the way silently up to what was now my sitting room and unlocked the door. Amina sank down on a leather pouf as soon as I'd closed the door. "I don't know what I'd have done if you hadn't come soon," she said wearily. "Mama's at her office, and I couldn't stay at home." She took off her dark glasses, and it was obvious that she'd been crying.

"What happened?" I demanded. "Your father didn't believe the story about the art exhibit?"

Amina nodded. "We had a terrible fight. The worst one ever. Meredith, you're lucky you're American. Papa is very modern, but he doesn't believe in daughters talking back to fathers."

"My father doesn't, either, if it makes you feel any better," I said.

Amina ignored that. She was crying again. I passed a box of tissues to her silently and she blew her nose hard. "It was terrible. I've never seen him so angry. It wasn't just because I lied. He said the most terrible things about Ali, and—and he said I mustn't ever speak to him again.

Not speak to him, or see him. Meredith, I'll die. You have to help me."

"Amina, it's not like I know Ali or anything, but maybe your father's right," I said as tactfully as I could.

"It wouldn't matter," Amina went on miserably. "He's a *part* of me. I *believe* in him, even if—" She choked on a sob. "Papa said if I even try to see him, or talk to him, or write, he'll send me off to my grandmother in Beirut and make me wear a veil! Oh, he won't really," she went on, wiping her eyes. "Papa thinks being in Lebanon is too dangerous, and he goes through hell worrying because Grandmama and Grandpapa refuse to leave. Their condo's been bombed twice, and— Oh, Meredith, I'm so sorry! I forgot about your uncle being there—"

"Never mind Mark right now," I said huskily. "What did you mean I have to help you?"

Amina caught my hands. "Meredith, I have to see Ali, to explain, to tell him things— If I could tell Papa that I'm with you, if I could even see Ali here— Papa wouldn't find out, I promise."

"No way." I shook my head. "I don't like lying, and besides it hardly ever works. I thought you found that out. Oh, Amina, *please.*"

Amina flung herself across the sofa in a flood of weeping. I knelt beside her, feeling helpless and vaguely guilty, hugging her and handing her one tissue after another. Presently she straightened.

"You're right," she said at last in a low whisper. "It's bad enough I get myself in trouble. I shouldn't try to drag you in it with me." She took a deep breath and turned to me. Most of her makeup was gone, and she looked at once younger and oddly older. "You are a good friend, Meredith. You do have the third eye. If there is ever anything that I can do for you. . . ."

I came to a decision. "You can. We've been getting these funny phone calls here, where nobody talks on the other end. And there's always this sort of hollow, rhythmic noise in the background." I demonstrated, as well as I was able. "I thought the noise might be a clue about who's calling. Or where the call is coming from. And if the calls are coming from Lebanon—you know a lot about the Middle East, on account of all your relatives there, don't you? Will you try to think of what those noises might be?"

Amina nodded thoughtfully. She left soon afterward, and I sat wondering whether my impulse to confide in her had been the right one.

·12·

Those first few days in Istanbul set the pattern for all the days to come. They began early, with rosy dawn gilding the view across the Bosphorus, and the *muezzin*'s call sounding mysteriously from the nearest mosque.

> . . . *Come to prayer;*
> *Come to salvation!*
> *God is most great!*
> *There is no god but Allah!*

Those calls—just before dawn, just after noon, in late afternoon, just after sunset, and after nightfall—marked the passing of time; made me aware of the fervently held beliefs underlying and permeating every detail of Muslim life. Of my life, too, so long as I was here.

Within these constants, the pattern of the summer took shape. Visits to Felicity from her obstetrician; visits from Dr. Koc, half professional, half social. My ever-present awareness of the servants—both of ours, and those Dr. Koc frequently sent over to assist us. And always, like a recurring dark motif, a growing conviction that things were not right.

Mark did not call again. There was only one more of those heavy-breathing callers, late one night. But twice, when I answered the telephone's ringing, a hoarse male voice asked for Mark Greystoke and hung up quickly when I said he wasn't there and asked who was calling.

Rachel and Matt went to a kind of summer day camp twice a week at the Anglican Church School. Friends of Felicity came to visit—Dr. Koc and her husband; Edith Hibborn and her husband, Herbert, who was stout and graying; the friends who had helped Felicity to set up her sitting room, Tom Truscott and Will Sheldon. They, and Mr. Hibborn, turned out to be colleagues of Mark's from the Institute for Nonviolent Intercession as well as members of the Greystokes' Quaker Meeting. They all spoke vaguely but reassuringly about Mark's continuing absence.

I saw Amina frequently, but we didn't speak about her boyfriend Ali. I could tell she was desperately in love—or was it desperate *and* in love—and there wasn't a darn thing I could say. And I saw Brandon almost all the time. He came over; he took me out, or me and the kids; sometimes he even took Matt and Rachel out without me, when I was busy with Felicity or Amina. We went swimming; we went out for dinner and dancing; we watched TV (no references to Mark—was that good or bad?). We never did get around to going to Topkapi Palace, or the Blue Mosque or Santa Sophia, or the Grand Bazaar. Somehow, living in Stamboul, we forgot that we were also tourists.

All at once two weeks had gone by, and Felicity's birthday was two days away. "That settles it. We'll go to the Grand Bazaar tomorrow," Brandon said when Matt reminded him of this. Matt had his allowance, plus loose change he'd won from Brandon playing cards. The money was definitely burning holes in Matt's pockets.

"I have ten dollars," Rachel contributed. "I've been saving up. I want to get Mommy something for the baby."

It came to me with a start that I hadn't seen any baby things in the house. Felicity probably had hand-me-downs from Matt and Rachel packed away somewhere. Or did she? They hadn't lived in Stamboul when Matt was born, and she'd had miscarriages since. Was Felicity holding off on buying baby things for fear something would happen?

Or for fear something would happen to Mark, and she'd have to return to the States before the baby came? The thought struck me out of nowhere.

I'll buy something for the baby tomorrow, too, I resolved. It would be an act of faith.

Brandon left, saying he'd come for us at nine the next morning.

I went into the kitchen to talk to Fatma about some kind of birthday meal for Felicity. Perhaps the Farkases and Brandon could come over.

"I take care of," Fatma said flatly.

"It won't be too much work? We'd have to eat upstairs, in Mrs. Greystoke's sitting room. Will there be room?"

"*I* take care. You do not worry," Fatma repeated. She was slapping sheets of phyllo dough out on the kitchen table. A carefully balanced truce existed between us, but she still wasn't thrilled about my invading her kitchen.

The doorbell rang. "I'll get it," I said quickly.

Fatma wiped her hands on a towel and jerked off her apron. "*I* answer. Bad enough you go when that Kamil is not here, or when your *friend* come." She'd long since made it clear she did not approve of Brandon's frequent visits. Since Brandon and Amina had been to the house already, her tone implied, whoever was on the doorstep now was *real* company. A servant must greet them to uphold the honor of the house. She stomped out and I sat on a kitchen stool dipping into the nut-and-honey filling for the pastries.

Almost immediately, Fatma reappeared. "Dr. Burlingame from the Anglican School. He want to see you. I put him in sitting room where he belong. Mr. Greystoke always see him in study. I bring coffee," she added, filling a kettle noisily.

I got out of there fast, leaving her to her standards of etiquette.

Dr. Burlingame was a gray Englishman—light gray suit, gray hair and slight beard, tired gray eyes. He rose as I entered, holding out an elderly hand. "Miss—I'm sorry, I don't recall your name, but I know you're Felicity Greystoke's niece and looking after her. Mark told me that Felicity must not be upset, so I had to see you."

"Something's happened to Mark!"

"No. That is—my dear young lady, please don't be alarmed, but I must ask you. Have you heard anything, anything at all, from Mark Greystoke?"

"Not for two weeks." I swallowed. "Why?"

"Then you don't know how to get in touch with him? We were hoping he'd left some message, some chain of contacts."

"No, he did not. Felicity would have told me, because she's not allowed to use the telephone." I clenched my hands together. "I know he's gone underground," I said carefully. "And I know what's been on TV in the States, my mother told me. But there hasn't been any news lately."

"Exactly. That is why . . . it is very important that I get in touch with him. . . ."

Dr. Burlingame looked at me with indecision, and I looked straight back. We were getting nowhere.

Fatma came in with a heavy brass tray. Coffeepot, coffee cups, plate of elaborate pastries, bowl of figs and almonds. She set it on the table by the right banquette and exited, her black skirt swishing.

"Please sit down," I said automatically. I poured the coffee and passed a cup and pastries. Going through the ritual motions steadied me. "You'd better tell me why you're so anxious to get in touch with my uncle. In case he calls."

Dr. Burlingame looked at me over the steaming cup. Then, almost as if we were in an espionage movie, he set it down, and reached in his inside jacket pocket, and took out a European-style wallet. Meticulously, he selected several cards of identity and laid them out. Stanley Lewis Burlingame, D.D., Ph.D. Anglican priest. Teacher of English and religion, Anglican School of Istanbul, Turkey. Associate, Institute for Nonviolent Intercession. I felt as though I should get my passport to prove I was really me.

"I regret the necessity for bringing you into this," Dr. Burlingame said. "But I really must. Word has come to me through . . . well, perhaps I shouldn't tell you through what route, except that the sources were very high and close to Ten Downing Street and the Oval Office. Mark must get out of Lebanon immediately. As soon as he can possibly arrange it. 'The usual supports and back-up cannot be provided this time.' Those were the exact words. You must remember them and repeat them accurately the very next time Mark calls. To him, and only to him. Do you understand?"

I nodded. My mouth was dry. "He hasn't called. He may not be able to—"

"I think he will," Dr. Burlingame interrupted quietly. "Felicity's birthday is in a day or so, I believe."

"There have—" I wet my lips and tried again. "There *have* been calls. Not from him, at least not directly. Calls with nobody there except heavy breathing and some kind of hollow sound effect in the background. Calls asking for Mark and hanging up without identification when I say he isn't here."

Dr. Burlingame frowned. "What have you told them?"

"Nothing. Except to ask who's calling, that is. Fatma curses them out if she answers the phone. We haven't told Felicity."

"Excellent. Give out no information to anyone, unless you hear Mark's voice. And I would not speak of what I've told you to anyone here." He meant it as a command, I knew. "If your uncle calls, and you have any sense that anyone else is listening . . . it would be as well to phrase the message that I gave you in other terms, ones which only your uncle would understand."

Our eyes locked in a silent covenant.

Dr. Burlingame reached with neat precision for a pastry. "Excellent," he murmured. "There are some things, thankfully, which never change." He finished the pastry and the cup of coffee. And he went, leaving me with my head whirling.

·13·

Ten Downing Street meant the British prime minister. The Oval Office meant the White House. I wasn't involved in politics, but I knew that much. Somebody high up knew what Mark was doing and had said he had to drop everything fast, and get out, because it wasn't safe. *The usual back-up couldn't be provided.*

What back-up? What kind of support was "usually" provided?

Sources close to the Oval Office. The secretary of state? The Pentagon? The CIA? *No,* my mind cried out. Mark wouldn't be part of anything that involved the CIA or the military.

Suppose I didn't really know Mark after all? Suppose the Institute for Nonviolent Intercession was a—what did the CIA call it? A cover, for a U.S. agency.

Mark, Mark, Mark, what have you gotten into? Gotten us all into? I cried out silently.

Two things were very clear. Mark was in great danger. And I must trust no one. *No one.*

I didn't tell Felicity about Dr. Burlingame's visit, even though I could have passed it off as a social call. I didn't call Brandon, though I longed to. And that night after the household was in bed, I sat for a long time with my hand on the receiver, trying to make my fingers dial my parents' number, and then took my hand away. How could I even be sure this telephone wasn't bugged?

Mark was, after all, being denounced in Turkey as an agent of Yankee imperialists and the CIA. *Anybody* could have bugged us. Even the CIA.

I went to bed, but I didn't sleep. In the morning I put on almost as much makeup as Amina wore, to camouflage that fact. And when Brandon arrived by taxi to collect Matt and Rachel, who were flying high with anticipation, I went with them and acted as if nothing in the world were wrong.

Fortunately, nobody noticed I was putting on an act. Matt and Rachel were too psyched up over visiting the bazaar. I invited Brandon to the family celebration for Felicity's birthday the next night, and he seemed very pleased at being included.

I had no idea what the Grand Bazaar would be like, but I certainly never imagined how large it was. Or how dark. Or how grand, in its front reaches, and ghetto-dismal and damp in the rear. It lay across the Galata Bridge, in one of the old reaches of Stamboul, and I felt as though we'd left all European influences behind.

"This isn't the Grand Bazaar," Rachel said, amused, as we passed the first open shops with their embroidered dresses and brass pots and trays. "This is just the lead-up. The real bazaar's up farther, under that roof. That's why its other name's the Covered Bazaar."

"Guess how many shops it has?" Matt demanded. And when Brandon and I just shook our heads he announced,

"More than four thousand! There are ninety-two streets, and they add up to forty miles."

"Which we're *not* going to walk all through," Brandon put in, correctly interpreting the gleam in Matt's eyes.

The taxi pulled up at a stone arch, and we got out.

It was overpowering. The size, the sounds, the stench . . . Always, I thought, I'll remember these smells. They were a mixture of the sweet, the savory and the sickening. Part department store (hair rollers, furniture polish, inexpensive T-shirts, name-brand cosmetics), part expensive boutiques (jewel-box jewelry stores displaying harem rings set with emeralds and rubies, and multi-million-dollar diamond necklaces), part Eastern bazaar (rugs, embroideries, brocades; copper, brass and silver; leather goods, furniture).

The shops in the front streets could have been in the finest part of Paris. Clients in custom-made clothing were being wooed with coffee in fine porcelain cups. As we penetrated deeper, the merchandise dropped in price and the streets became narrower and more crowded. Rachel shopped carefully, checking to be sure embroidery was hand done and haggling prices like a little old lady. Matt darted from one shop to another, torn between unnecessary but fascinating gadgets (for Felicity's present) and the lure of scimitars.

"You know what Daddy said," Rachel pointed out, sounding big-sisterish.

"Oh, shut up!" Matt shouted when he'd heard this for the fourth time. "Daddy's not here! For all we know—" He stopped abruptly.

Rachel glowered at him, and Matt quailed. "I think I'll get this for Mommy," she said loudly, holding a loose, embroidered cotton dress with a crocheted yoke out toward me. "Daddy likes Mommy in blue. Maybe I can get something blue for the baby to go with it."

"That sounds like a fine idea," I said steadily.

The shopkeeper hurried forward and he and Rachel haggled. Matt plunged off down the street.

"No, you don't, sport." Brandon plunged after him, and they disappeared from view around a far corner.

Rachel concluded her bargaining, and the shopkeeper ducked in back to wrap the purchases. He emerged with two neatly tied packages before Brandon and Matt returned. I looked down the street uncertainly, and Rachel caught my arm.

"We'd better stay here. It's easy to get lost in the bazaar. I hope Matt hasn't gone too far. Mommy doesn't like us to go down those back streets."

"Why not?" I asked.

Rachel gave a fastidious shrug. "They smell. The stuff back there's all junk, anyway. Of course, *Matt* thinks they're great. He pretends he's a foreign spy."

Her words hung in the air.

A family of German tourists squeezed into the little shop. "We'd better go out," I murmured to Rachel, and she nodded. We maneuvered our way out to the street.

"The boys will find us if we stay on the same street," Rachel said, taking my hand protectively. This was one of the inexpensive but respectable sections of the bazaar. We started sauntering slowly away from the back regions. I still had to buy my presents, I remembered. We found a shop of enchanting children's wear, and I bought a baby's cap and booties, and in a linen shop a round tablecloth for the table in Felicity's room where we now ate most nights.

It was midday now, and people were taking refuge from the outside heat in the bazaar. Rachel and I wandered on. I kept looking over my shoulder, watching for Matt and Brandon. Then I stiffened.

"Are they coming?" Rachel spun around.

"No, I—thought I saw them. But I didn't." It wasn't quite a lie. I had seen someone, but it had not been Brandon. It had been one of the youths whom I'd seen with Kamil, the one who worked for the Farkases. The one I'd seen Kamil strike in the street market.

As soon as Rachel's recognizably American voice had called out now, he had vanished. My eyes scanned the dimness of the covered street and saw only strangers.

"There you are!" That *was* Brandon, coming around a corner toward us. He reached us in seconds, holding Matt's left hand firmly. Both looked elated. Brandon was carrying several bundles, and in Matt's right hand—

"Matt! You know you weren't supposed to buy a scimitar!" I cried.

"You're going to get it," Rachel chimed in.

"Relax, both of you," Brandon said calmly. "Matt didn't buy it, I got it for him as a souvenir." He brandished the bundles with as much satisfaction as Matt waved the scimitar. "Matt spent all his ill-gotten gains on presents, so that makes it okay, doesn't it? I got a few good souvenirs, too. You were right, Meredith, the shopping's much better here than in the Beyoglu or Taksim districts."

"Don't 'You were right' me, not when—" I shut up quickly as startled heads turned toward me. We were in sight of the bazaar's main entrance now, and the window shoppers were decidedly upscale. Brandon let go of Matt's hand and Matt charged ahead, flourishing his brass-sheathed sword above his head. Rachel followed. I turned on Brandon.

"Not when you know his parents are pacifists. When I *told* you they don't want him to have weapons."

"Oh, come on, Meredith," Brandon said tolerantly. "That thing's just a toy! It couldn't kill anybody—it would probably snap in two first, it's so cheap. If you're worried, I'll dull the blade, or Kamil can."

Was it his tone of tolerance that fueled my fire? "That's not the point! The point is—"

"The point," Brandon retorted in a swift, low whisper, "is that Matt's a kid whose father's missing in a lousy, bloody, no-win religious war, leaving an eight-year-old thinking he has to be the man of the house. Half of him wants to stay a kid playing glorious games, the other half is scared stiff he won't be able to protect his mother and sister, not to mention you. Do you really think it's such a terrible sin to give him a toy scimitar for the sake of his morale?"

The cool logic was like a blow to me.

We had reached the main entrance arch, no place for a public quarrel. I forced my breathing to slow down to normal before stepping out. And then, just as I did so, Brandon, in an entirely different tone, muttered an oath.

I spun toward him, startled.

Brandon was staring at a pile of papers at a news kiosk.

The printing was foreign, but the prominent photo on the front page was all too familiar. The original hung, enlarged, in the Greystokes' sitting room. A family group—Mark, Felicity, Rachel, Matt.

"What does it say?" I exclaimed, forgetting Brandon could not read Turkish.

"Not now." Brandon flung some coins to the news vendor, rolled a paper swiftly under his arm, and dove for the children, who had already stepped outside. I followed.

For a minute I could not believe what I was seeing.

The arched entrance faced an open area where, when we had arrived, trucks and taxis and pushcarts had been jostling. Now the traffic had been nearly stopped by demonstrators. All of them were men, Turkish or Arab, mostly wearing Arab *kaffiyeh* headdresses. They were chanting, shouting, brandishing signs on poles. Most of the signs I couldn't read, but the others—

Yankee Imperialists . . . CIA . . . Greystoke . . .

And the picture from the paper.

"Come on, sport!" Brandon grabbed Matt and swooped him up beneath one long arm.

The crowd surged toward us. In a minute, Brandon and Matt were swept from sight. Then Rachel, too, disappeared. A van rolled up, disgorging a TV camera. I'd never seen an actual TV camera, but I knew that was what this was.

I couldn't find Rachel.

I'd never been so terrified in my life.

And then a voice, a perfectly natural, very feminine voice, called to me in Turkish. I didn't recognize the words but I knew the voice, knew the bubbling tone and knew it was assumed. Amina. Amina, hurrying toward me with a tall, handsome, dark young man behind her. They pushed through the crowd as though it weren't even there. Ali—it had to be Ali—swung Rachel up in his arms and by instinct she hid her face against his shoulder. He flagged a cab and dumped Rachel into it, found Brandon and pulled Matt from him.

Amina pushed me into the cab and held out her arms for Matt. Ali swung him in beside us and slammed the door. Amina gave a sharp order in Turkish and the cab screeched off, leaving Brandon and Ali among the crowd.

"You can talk to him later. Just keep quiet. We're going to my mother's office," Amina said tightly.

None of us said a word till we were there, in the air-conditioned, polished-wood safety of Dr. Koc's private consulting room. The receptionist took the children somewhere to get cleaned up and have soft drinks, and I looked at Amina and started to shake.

"Thank you. I don't know what to say. If you hadn't been there . . . But why *were* you there with—"

Amina's hand shot up and she jerked her head warningly at the wall separating us from Dr. Koc and a patient. "I told you I had to—you know. Allah and our third eyes must have sent us there this morning."

I agreed fervently. "Those posters—the newspapers—what did they say?"

Amina shrugged. "More of the usual. Nothing new about where your uncle is. You sit here and catch your breath. I'm going to have the receptionist phone the limousine service Papa uses. We'll go home hidden by dark window glass, in case we pass any more demonstrators."

The ride home was peaceful. And everything at the house was peaceful, astonishingly so. We all told Felicity we'd had a great time at the bazaar, and none of us betrayed by the flicker of an eyelash that anything had gone wrong. Neither Matt nor Rachel said a word to me about it, either. I didn't know whether that was good or bad.

I let Matt sleep that night with the scimitar beside his bed. Sometime between night and morning, Rachel crept into bed beside me, and I let her stay.

And no one called. Not our anonymous callers. Not Brandon. Not Mark.

·14·

Several things happened the next morning. Felicity asked whether Mark had called. I said no, but that didn't prove anything was wrong. Felicity said she knew that. Edith Hibborn phoned to find out if we knew about the newspapers.

"It was nothing new, just the usual rumors. Not to worry. Do the children know?"

I told her what had happened yesterday at the Grand Bazaar.

"Most unfortunate. I think you'd better keep them under wraps till things get sorted out. This is their day for summer camp, isn't it? Perhaps they should go daily for a while; Dr. Burlingame will keep them sheltered. I'll drive them over in my auto, shall I? Nonsense, it's no trouble. I'd like to wish Felicity a happy birthday, anyway."

Her unflappability was like a lifeline. She brought Felicity a large bouquet of flowers, and I arranged them in a blue glass bowl.

Dr. Koc came next, to check on Felicity and also on me. "I feel so awful about what happened to the children," I confessed. "I never should have risked taking them."

"Nonsense," Dr. Koc said briskly. "One has to carry on with a normal life, or one develops a siege mentality. Neither Mark nor Felicity would want that. May I say something? Though you're Mark's niece, and Rachel and Matthew are his children, you're probably more shaken by what happened than they are. They've lived with their father's work all their lives. They're used to the reality."

I remembered what Brandon had been saying to me, just before all hell broke loose.

Brandon didn't call, but Amina did, shortly after her mother left. "I hear the children have gone out. Good. I'm taking you out, too."

"I really don't—"

"Wear something that covers you up. I'll pick you up in five minutes. Nobody's going to recognize *you* from that photograph."

Amina took me to the Blue Mosque. We left our shoes with those of many others on the outer steps, Amina discreetly nudging me into the proper protocol. Barefoot and a bit uneasy, I stepped in—onto Oriental rugs, piled one on another, as far as eye could see. Pattern on pattern, color on color . . . There was pattern on pattern on the wall tiles, too, but the overwhelming color was blue. Dark blue on light, in swirling calligraphy, in geometric forms— circles, spirals, arches, what looked like Stars of David, and twelve-pointed stars. Islam did not believe in "graven images," so all of the patterns were abstract.

The mosque was huge, and shadowy, and still. The carpets were being walked soundlessly now by hundreds of bare feet. I wondered how many more had trodden them through the years. Tourists wandered in tight groups, but most of the worshipers were men. They faced toward Mecca, standing, then kneeling, then prostrating themselves on those velvet rugs, in turn. Far to one side, I saw a young father teaching his toddler son the prayer ritual. A lump formed in my throat.

It was so foreign to church as I was used to it, yet what struck me most was a sense of rightness and of peace. It reminded me, oddly, of a Quaker service I'd been to once with Mark. People had sat in decorous, orderly silence and waited till someone felt moved to speak. ("What are they waiting for?" I'd asked Mark in a whisper. Mark had scribbled a note and passed it back: "For God to give them what to say.") The feel here was the same. I wondered suddenly if that was what had drawn Mark into a "ministry of reconciliation," as he called it, in the Middle East.

Amina touched my arm. "Let's tag on with this tour group." The guide was of indeterminate age, and thin, with the dusty, long-jacketed black suit worn by many Muslim men. He whisked us from one area to another amid a constant low babble of broken English. I heard words about the spiral of breath to God and from God, about the Five Pillars of Islam, about God being "nearer to man than his neck vein." About journeys to Mecca, and the wonders of experiencing God. Some of the tourists in our group looked away, embarrassed by this fervor. I glanced sideways at Amina. She was still, gazing into the middle distance, an unreadable expression on her face.

The guide, his black eyes eager, opened a guidebook to a photo of the Great Mosque at Mecca, and the Black Stone, a meteorite that was one of Islam's most hallowed objects. He whipped a dog-eared snapshot from his wallet—himself, before the Black Stone. "You Jew? You Christian? You know Abraham? He go here. You Jew, you Christian, I Moslem, we all children of Abraham. Abraham, Jesus, Muhammad, they all testify to Allah. 'The Lord our God, the Lord is One.'"

For some reason, I turned away slightly. And as I did, I became aware of some disruption in the atmosphere. Alien, but not unfamiliar.

I looked around quickly.

Something—someone—moved out of sight behind a nearby pillar. But as I stared, and then went over boldly to look closer, there was no one there.

I walked dazedly off to one side, feeling weak.

After a minute Amina touched my arm. "Are you all right? You look very pale."

"Fine. Something just—" My throat closed before I could get the words out.

Amina's eyes scanned mine, but she let that pass. "We'd better be going," she said. "It's getting hot out, and you have the birthday dinner to get ready for."

I didn't have that much to do, for Fatma had taken everything out of my hands, but I wanted to get out of there. It was time to get back anyway. Amina came in with me and stayed for lunch, and Fatma told me "Your friend called."

I felt myself blushing. "Is he calling back?"

"No need. He ask what time dinner, and I tell him."

So at least Brandon was still coming. But the memory of our sudden quarrel, short but deep, about the scimitar still hung between us.

Amina and Felicity and I had lunch in Felicity's sitting room. Rachel had called to ask permission for her and Matt to stay for lunch and the afternoon at the Anglican School, helping Dr. Burlingame decorate for some event or other. In midafternoon Amina went home. The house was still.

The mail had arrived, bringing cards and notes and packages for Felicity. Nothing that could have come from Mark. I sorted the mail carefully, and took what was not likely to be disturbing upstairs. I hung around Felicity's room while she opened gifts and read her birthday cards. Packages had come from my parents, and from Gran and Gramp. The cards were funny, and the notes written on them were upbeat. The family was being careful, and my grandfather had even restrained himself from saying "I told you so."

"Nothing from Mark," Felicity said. "That's as I expected. When you're in a lot of neighborhoods or small towns in this part of the world, even if you're not keeping a low profile, it's difficult to get anything mailed. If you can get hold of anything *to* mail."

"I guess finding a *To My Wife* birthday card in English in Lebanon right now could be a hopeless cause." I was trying to be light and casual, but those last words had an unintentional resonance to them.

Felicity decided to take a long shower before dressing for the party. I went to the kitchen to see how things were going, and got thrown out. Great vases of flowers adorned all the rooms, and Kamil was carefully misting the plants around the fountain. He disappeared as soon as I came through. The kids had come home and were on the upper gallery, playing cards. "How are you guys doing?" I asked, and Rachel answered "Fine," absently.

They were seemingly unshaken by yesterday's events at the bazaar. I was afraid to bring the subject up with the kids for fear of opening a can of worms I couldn't handle. I hoped they'd had a chance to talk about it with Dr. Burlingame, who was better equipped to cope.

I went to my room, shut the door, and lay down, staring at the ceiling. What I saw there was a shifting montage of memory pictures. The newspaper kiosk at the bazaar, and the shock of seeing the family's picture in the paper. The signs the demonstrators brandished. The hate on their faces as they looked at us.

I'd never seen real fanaticism before. Oh, I'd heard about it. I'd seen it on TV. But this was different. It was hard for me to understand the *us and them* mentality involved; the desire for confrontation, not for peace. I wished desperately that Mark were there to tell us everything would be all right, to make sense out of senseless things.

And I wished desperately I could still believe, as I always had, that Mark *could* make things all right.

When I couldn't stand my thoughts any more I took a shower, dressed carefully, and went downstairs to be ready to greet our guests.

Fatma had produced a many-course feast, and we all exerted ourselves to do it, and Felicity, justice. The Farkas family arrived dressed to the teeth and glittering with jewels, carrying gifts in spite of the fact that they'd already sent an arrangement of orchids. Brandon came at the same time as they did, which made things less strained between us, and he, too, brought flowers. Matt, who was wound up, ran up ahead of the others with the gifts. Rachel showed everyone up to where Felicity was waiting in her sitting room, which was garlanded with flowers and lit with antique oil lamps.

It was a magical evening, an evening outside of time—back somewhere in the days of old Byzantium. Before all the trouble started, I thought, and then remembered there had never been such a time. Not in two thousand years.

What Brandon was thinking I didn't know. Amina was being very much the *femme fatale,* talking and laughing a little too much, and I could have killed her. There was a lot I needed to work out with Brandon, there was a lot I needed to ask Amina. But I couldn't, not with the others there.

It was midnight before the party broke up. By then Fatma had bundled the kids off to bed. Felicity was concealing yawns. I went downstairs with the guests, and since Kamil was once more nowhere around, I let them out.

Brandon lingered and turned to face me when the others had gone. "Ali showed up in the nick of time yesterday," he said quietly.

"I know. He's good in a crisis, even though I'm not so sure he's good for Amina," I admitted.

"Inside knowledge or intuition?" Brandon teased.

"Don't."

"Don't what?"

"Start on that. Intuition."

Brandon said "Oh," softly. Then he leaned against the

door and put his hand over mine. "Meredith," he said gently, "don't you think it's time you put your 'intuition' to one side and started facing facts?"

"About what? Are you talking about demonstrators and giving little kids weapons to play with? If you want to talk about facing reality, *you're* the one who tried to whisk me past the TV set that night at the Sheraton. Your Western rationalism wasn't much help in getting us past the demonstrators, if you come right down to it!"

I was being unfair, and I knew it. Brandon whitened. "If I'd had time to learn the Middle Eastern mindset, like I'm trying to, my 'rationalism' might have done us some good. Yes, I stood there feeling helpless! Yes, I'm glad your Muslim friends showed up! Is that what you want to hear? It doesn't cancel out the fact that you and the Greystokes are in the middle of an incredibly dangerous situation, and a little less idealism and a little more realism about weapons for self-protection might save your lives!"

"Mark and Felicity don't believe that, and neither do I!"

"Mark," Brandon said carefully, "might not come back, or hasn't that occurred to you yet? Don't you think you'd better face that possibility?"

"What I think," I said in a furious whisper, "is that I made a mistake trusting my instincts about *you*. You said you admired Mark Greystoke's work—what he stood for—"

"I do. But admiring and sticking your head in the sand like an ostrich to avoid reality are two different things."

"Not to me!"

Brandon just looked at me and shrugged, and then he let himself out. I barred the door and turned to go up to bed, feeling absolutely awful.

The telephone rang.

I picked it up, and again I heard that breathing. And the rhythmic sound in the background. I didn't say anything. I just stood waiting, knowing the silent caller knew I was there, and after several minutes the line went dead.

·15·

The next day was incredibly calm. I was glad, because my argument with Brandon loomed large in my thoughts. It was an effort to focus on anything else.

Felicity was feeling great, humming as she settled her presents into place. Gran had sent a huge package of yarns in pale pastels, plus knitting needles and crochet hooks and instructions for making baby things. *Have faith and get busy:* The message was unmistakable. Gran had also sent one of her famous cross-stitch samplers, beautifully framed.

> *God grant me the serenity*
> *To accept the things I cannot change,*
> *Courage to change the things I can,*
> *And the wisdom to know*
> *One from the other.*

"I remember that from Gran's kitchen," I said nostalgically.

"So do I." Felicity grinned. "It was written by a man named Reinhold Niebuhr. It's also the Alcoholics Anonymous prayer. I guess I should do something positive, shouldn't I?" And she started knitting a very small pink sweater. She pointed to the yarn when she told us all that she'd known the results of her amniocentesis for some time; the baby was a girl. It was the first sign she'd given of believing this child would live.

My grandparents, being nobody's fools, had also sent a box of very involved card and board games, suited to keep children's minds off troubling subjects. The games occupied the kids after they got home from day camp, and I joined them.

Brandon didn't call for two days. When he did, I wasn't home and Fatma took the message. He left the phone number for me to return the call. I didn't. He called again later in the week, and I spoke noncommittally and got off the phone quickly, saying we had company. We did — Edith Hibborn and her husband — but they were upstairs with Felicity. I tried to convince myself that I was sticking to my principles, but I had an empty feeling in my stomach.

The Hibborns stayed for dinner, and afterwards we all played one of the new games together. I liked the Hibborns; they were down to earth and unpretentious and fun and wise. Mr. Hibborn told stories about his grandchildren, and drew Matt and Rachel out about happenings at their day camp. "Dr. Burlingame tells me you're really something on the soccer field," he said to Matt's delight, and turned to me. "You haven't visited the institute yet, young lady. Why don't you come by tomorrow afternoon for tea?"

"I'd like that," I said. So the next afternoon, after the kids had returned from day camp and we'd had a late lunch, after Felicity was engrossed in knitting the pink sweater and the kids and games were spread out on the roof, I walked to the next corner and hailed a taxi.

The Institute for Nonviolent Intercession was in the international quarter of Stamboul. I'd driven by it in a cab with Amina. It was of pale yellowish-cream stone, two stories high, rather like a bank with louvered blinds at the plate-glass windows and the name carved in the arch above the door in Turkish, Arabic, French, and English. It was tucked in between a bank and a couple of consulates. So I knew a block before we reached it that we were getting close.

I could tell from the way the taxi slowed, the way a couple of vans were parked at odd angles so the street was narrowed to a single lane, that something was going on.

"You can stop here," I told the taxi driver, and paid him and got out. The sun was hot, so I had on a sunhat and the dark sunglasses I'd bought. I squeezed my way around the right-hand van, and then I saw.

Demonstrators. I thought they were picketing one of the consulates. Then I saw the signs.

Signs on poles, brandished in fists held high above *kaffiyeh*-wrapped heads (the men were Arabs, not Turks, my mind registered automatically). Pictures of Mark and the family. Pictures of Mark alone.

I couldn't get away because the crowd closed around me, carrying me forward toward the institute. My feet couldn't have moved me one way or the other. I saw the institute's front door open, and Mr. Hibborn come out, calm and reasonable.

I saw a black-clad arm come up out of the mob in front of him, and swing. As if throwing a baseball overhand.

Only it was no baseball. The thing arched up and forward, and came down. Into a group of people who suddenly began to scatter. Onto the sidewalk—I could only guess that, for I couldn't see it. I heard a sound like a firecracker, and then I saw fire. Fire, and black smoke, and then pieces of things hurtling through the air.

And then there was a stillness. I saw fragments of shattered glass around the edges of the institute's window frames, and on my arms and in my hair. And I saw a little empty space, and in that space a young woman sitting on the curb, hugging herself and moaning. An old woman, dressed in dusty black, lying face down on the sidewalk, looking as though her right leg was doubled under her. Except her right leg wasn't there.

A sensible shoe, with a foot in it, lying incongruously in the road.

Mr. Hibborn lying in the road, looking so peaceful except for a great gash in his head. Mrs. Hibborn kneeling beside him, tearing off her blouse to wrap around the gash. I knew it wasn't any use. I knew he was dead.

I knew I had to get back home. If there were demonstrators here, what would I find back at the house?

I moved slowly, carefully, sliding through the crowd until I reached an open street. I found a cab, and jumped into it, forcing the address out through a dry mouth. "*Hurry!*" I added, and blessedly the driver understood English. We careened through side streets.

I knew before we reached the house that I was right. The demonstrators, and reporters with TV crews, had ferreted out Mark Greystoke's address. It was the same thing again—hauling out money, jumping from the cab, pushing forward—

My heart stood still. Two small, familiar figures had appeared near the rim of the roof. I heard the crash of breaking glass and saw a stone go through one of the second-story windows. As if in answer, Matt held up one of the roof's potted plants and dropped it with accuracy on a demonstrator's head.

Oh God, I prayed, don't let it be the whole same thing. Then my heart lurched. Felicity was on the roof, behind the children, dragging them back from sight. They disappeared just as a volley of stones went flying upward.

I pushed my way through the crowd, I don't know how. There was no use going to the front door. Then, like a sign from heaven, the Farkases' front door opened and Amina stood there. "Mer!" she called, and I ran to her. Amina pulled me in and slammed the door behind us. She stared at me. "You're hurt—your arm's bleeding—"

"It doesn't matter. The kids are on the roof—Felicity's up there—she must have run up two flights—"

"I'll call Papa," Amina said instantly. "You get over there."

"How?"

Amina pushed me into the Farkas kitchen and opened a door onto the alley between the houses. "There's a door into your dining room right over there. Didn't you ever notice?"

I shook my head dumbly. The dining room wall was heavily carved and paneled; the alley was visible only from the roof because at street level a high, locked gate closed it in. The back end opened into the Farkas garden, but I scarcely glanced in that direction. I threw myself at the door of our house and banged and banged, until at last

Kamil came and opened it. Then I ran right past him. Into the courtyard, up the first flight of stairs, the second—

And then I screamed. Because Felicity lay in a heap of violet-colored caftan at the foot of the iron stairs from the roof. She lay on the tile floor, with her eyes closed and a gash reminding me of Mr. Hibborn's on her head. The blood seeped out, dark red, onto the tiles and onto Rachel's pale blue dress.

·16·

"Where's Matt?" I demanded shrilly, running over.

Rachel lifted a tear-streaked face. "Calling Dr. Koc's office."

"Good. What—what happened?"

"I don't *know!* They were throwing things—and then Matt threw that flowerpot." Rachel gulped. "I couldn't get him to come away, and then Mom—Mom—tripped on her caftan—"

"I know, darling." I was feeling frantically for Felicity's pulse. It was pounding in her neck. Thank God.

Then Amina was there. "Papa's called the police," she said in a low voice. "And the American Consulate. He's trying to get through to the institute."

"He won't," I said harshly, and told her what had happened. Amina grew very still.

Dr. Koc rushed in, carrying her medical bag. She sent Amina to get water. Distantly, I heard police sirens. Maybe ambulance sirens, too; I wasn't sure. I discovered with surprise that I was shaking all over. I knelt there hugging my chest to hold myself together.

Amina returned with water. By now Felicity was conscious and struggling to sit up. Dr. Koc held her down.

"The kids are okay," I said swiftly. "The police are out front."

"Thank God." Felicity sank back.

Ambulance attendants came pounding up the stairs, followed by Rachel and Matt and Mr. Farkas.

"Not the hospital!" Felicity said sharply. Her glance fell on the children and turned to me with panic.

"I know," I said. I signaled to Rachel and Matt to go away. They obeyed, their eyes wide and frightened.

Felicity's hands were gripping Dr. Koc's sleeves. "Tell me what happened, quickly," Dr. Koc said. "No, not you, Felicity." I told her, and Dr. Koc went on checking Felicity over all the while.

"I guess you'll live," Dr. Koc said at last. "Not that you deserve to! Really, Felicity, after all my lectures!"

"This was an emergency," Felicity said flatly.

"The baby's all right," Dr. Koc said. "You may have a concussion, but no broken bones." She and I exchanged a long, thoughtful look. The same thought was in both our minds: Here in her own house was the only place Felicity wws likely to be insulated from news of Mark.

"I'll let you stay here," Dr. Koc told Felicity at last, "only so long as nothing else goes wrong. Understand?"

Felicity nodded. The ambulance attendants Mr. Farkas had summoned carried her down and put her to bed. Dr. Koc sewed up her wound—without anesthetic, because Felicity was afraid it might harm the baby. She was exhausted by now, so we tiptoed out of her room and closed the door. The ambulance crew left. I leaned against the doorframe feeling drained.

"The police are waiting downstairs to talk to you," Mr.

Farkas reminded me. I looked at him, and started to shake again, and burst into tears.

Amina took me in her arms and told her parents about the bombing at the institute. Dr. Koc wanted to give me a sedative. *"No!"* I said sharply, and followed Mr. Farkas downstairs. He brushed past the police and went straight to the telephone in Mark's study, and I followed. I don't know who he called, but he found out the facts about the bombing. The Sons of the Prophet were taking credit. Mr. Hibborn and the woman I'd seen were dead. Two other employees of the institute were wounded slightly. A lot of damage had been done in the front office, but little elsewhere. Mrs. Hibborn had returned to her own home, accompanied by friends.

I heard all this through a kind of haze. I stayed in that haze through the rest of the afternoon; Dr. Koc told Felicity gently about the demonstrations, the bombing, and Mr. Hibborn's death. She mentioned the Sons of the Prophet's involvement, omitting the charge that Mark was working for the CIA. The Farkases stayed with me while I was interviewed by first the police and then an official from the American consulate. Dr. Koc made it clear to everyone that Felicity knew nothing and must not be disturbed.

Finally everybody was gone except the Farkases. They wanted us to go back to their house for dinner. Rachel and Matt and I all refused. Amina wanted to stay over that night. I refused that, too. Dr. Koc and her husband exchanged glances. "This is Fatma's afternoon off, isn't it?" Dr. Koc asked. "She should be back soon."

I just nodded. I felt as if I were in a little gray fog. At

last they went. I was glad. I took the kids to the kitchen and gave them soft drinks, since it was too hot for tea, my mother's cure-all. They wanted to see their mother, but I said we'd better not disturb her. They didn't protest.

Fatma came home, almost spitting fire. She had heard what had happened and had herself encountered one of the demonstrations. She was so angry that I didn't need to convince her that nothing else should upset Felicity if we could avoid it.

Fatma fixed a supper tray for Felicity and bullied her into eating. I cooked hamburgers and french fries for the rest of us while Matt and Rachel made the salad. We ate in the kitchen, and we didn't talk much. Felicity was already asleep when we went upstairs.

I went to bed, still in my shroud of fog. I wasn't feeling anything, literally. I couldn't think. But I could not stop shaking. I stared at the ceiling and what I was seeing there, like a projection of a woodcut, was Mark's face. Even that didn't make me feel anything.

The next thing I knew Rachel was pulling at me, her voice sharp with fear. "Meredith! Meredith, wake up!"

I struggled up and snapped on the light. "What's wrong?"

"It's Mommy! She was ringing the bellpull—outside her door— Fatma didn't hear. Mommy's all doubled up, holding her stomach—"

I streaked from the bedroom without waiting for the rest.

Felicity was hunched on the gallery's tile floor, her face gray and damp. "Call Dr. el-Faisal!" I ordered Rachel, and she ran downstairs.

We waited endlessly until the doctor came. The ambulance, also summoned by Rachel, arrived with her. This time there was no fooling around or bargaining.

"I'm taking her to the American Hospital," Dr. el-Faisal said. "The staff will do all it can to keep her from hearing any rumors about her husband. I've already arranged for a private room. We'll pressure your embassy to supply a security guard."

She didn't offer to let me go along with them to the hospital, and I didn't ask to. My responsibility was with the children. Astonishingly, through all of this Matt hadn't waked up. Rachel and I spent the rest of the night together, huddled close for comfort.

"Is she going to lose the baby?" Rachel asked fearfully. I said I didn't know. In the morning I told Matt, who asked no questions. His face had settled into a miniature mask of his father's, remote and reserved. I made them go to day camp. It was better than their staying here unable to do anything to help. Better than them seeing me if I cracked up.

I called the hospital. The switchboard would give out no information. I found out when visiting hours started, and was there promptly. They wouldn't let me see Felicity. "I'll wait," I said grimly. Finally Dr. Koc came to the hospital. She saw Felicity, and then she came for me.

"She's all right, and she hasn't lost the baby."

"Will she?" I asked baldly.

"It's possible," Dr. Koc said frankly. "Felicity's late in her sixth month now. She went into premature labor, as you know, but Dr. el-Faisal was able to stop it. If we can prevent labor until the fetus is viable. . . ."

I nodded and used the telephone in Dr. Koc's office to telephone my mother. Mother had seen the pictures of the bombing and the demonstrations on TV and had been frantic when she'd called the house and gotten only Fatma speaking Turkish. I spent fifteen minutes convincing Mother that she mustn't come, that her presence would only alarm Felicity. I spent another fifteen minutes hearing the most recent stateside rumors regarding Mark and the Sons of the Prophet.

"Your father's calling our congresswoman to try to get more news," Mother reported.

I made what I hoped afterward were suitable replies. I didn't really know what I was saying. And then I took a taxi to pick up Matt and Rachel from day camp and told them everything I felt I should.

·17·

I saw Felicity the next day, finally, and she begged me not to tell Mark she was in the hospital. "When he calls, just tell him mother and baby are doing fine. Please, Meredith. I know you hate pretending, but Mark mustn't worry about us. His mission's too important. You can do that, can't you?"

"Sure, Felicity," I said huskily.

Felicity also wanted me to visit Mrs. Hibborn. "That poor woman. Seeing her husband killed before her eyes." Felicity's eyes darkened, and I knew she was thinking of the very real possibility it could happen to her.

If Mark didn't get killed by the Sons of the Prophet somewhere in Lebanon. Or wasn't dead already.

I called on Mrs. Hibborn that afternoon and found her at the institute, superintending the repairs of the ruined office. She was, as Felicity had predicted, valiant.

"Oh, my dear, all of us in the foreign service who work in trouble spots live with the knowledge this may happen. Felicity and Mark know that, too. Of course I'm going on with my work here. My husband would have expected that, and besides, I want to." She regarded me with wise, sad eyes. "My dear, may I say something? Don't try to protect Felicity overmuch, or the children either. Of course we all want to. But Felicity has an inner strength. I suspect you have it, too, though you may not believe it."

"I wish I could," I answered somberly.

"Why don't you bring the children to Meeting one of these Sundays? They haven't been since—oh, sometime before Mark left for Lebanon. We meet in homes, you know. I'll give you a list." She found a copy in one of the undamaged file cabinets. "Oh, I see we're supposed to be at your house Sunday after next. We'll make other arrangements."

"Don't. At least not till I've talked to Felicity about it."

I left feeling uneasily that she'd comforted me more than I had her.

I phoned Brandon that night, but his hotel switchboard said he was out of town. He would be back tomorrow. I chickened out when it came to leaving any message.

I saw Amina a lot that week. She was acting odd, alternately displaying that bright mask of chatter and then, as if she realized it was inappropriate in the circumstances, going somber. I had a feeling she was upset about Ali again. When I asked, she said he was away for a couple of days, and anyway her father was still being totally impossible. That was as much as I got from her.

Matt was involved in soccer, and Rachel had joined a swim team at the day camp and was doing so well that Mark would be very proud when he came home.

We were all of us going through the motions of normal lives; we were all acting as if we were sealed up inside glass jars side by side on the same shelf.

One thing I did do; I reinstituted the family prayers that Felicity and the children always had together. I felt uncomfortable doing so, because they'd never been part of my family's traditions. But I felt a responsibility, somehow, and it turned out easier than I thought because the kids accepted it so matter-of-factly. I had the kids each look up some passage of Scripture to read each night, and I did also. We gathered in Felicity's room and read aloud; it made her seem closer. And we held hands and said the familiar prayers, and any other prayers Matt or Rachel felt like saying. I didn't do that; I felt too shy, but I prayed inside.

The day after Brandon was supposed to come back to Istanbul, a large bouquet of flowers arrived. With it was a note for me. "I read about what happened. I'm so sorry. Can I take you & kids out for dinner somewhere tomorrow night? Or if you can't leave Felicity I'll bring the food to your house. No arguments, I promise."

I showed the note to Amina and she said I'd be a fool if I didn't go. "Ask Felicity. She'd say the same thing."

"Felicity doesn't know about the scimitar."

"Oh, don't be so stubborn!" Amina retorted. "You think one souvenir sword's going to turn Mark Greystoke's son into a killing machine? If you don't phone that gorgeous man and accept his invitation, I'll do it for you!"

"Don't you dare!"

After Amina left I phoned, rationalizing it was for the children's sake. Brandon, to my mixed disappointment and relief, wasn't there. I left a message: My aunt wasn't well enough to accept the invitation, but the other three of us would be ready for him to pick us up at six-thirty.

I told Amina, just to prove my open-mindedness, and Amina said she was glad to hear I was using some sense at last. She herself was going to a concert with her parents tomorrow night, but I was to call her first thing the next morning and let her know how things went.

I knew Matt would be glad to see Brandon again, but I was surprised, as the hours of the next day passed, to find how my own spirits were rising. I almost forgot about all the horrors.

Of course, I would be taking two little chaperones along on my date. But that was good, too, because it meant Brandon and I couldn't get into any confrontations.

The whole evening, in fact, seemed like something straight out of a "happy family" type of TV sitcom. Brandon had been to Syria, and he'd brought back souvenirs. A doll for Rachel's collection; a complicated board game for Matt. "Nothing that will lead you into trouble, kiddo, unless you find a way to play that for money too!"

That was his only reference to our quarrel. His gift for me was open to interpretation. Worry beads, a chain of amber ones.

"Of course, gold would have been a better match for your eyes, but that's out of my league. Anyway, amber stands for healing." Brandon turned to the waiter and gave our orders. He'd taken us to the coffee shop at the Hilton, which meant we could get plain old American short-order food. We had cheeseburgers and french fries and milk shakes, and sundaes for dessert. It was so much like home.

We got back to the house early. "Can I come in?" Brandon asked.

"I think you'd better not."

"Whatever you want." It wasn't what I wanted, but what I thought was the best idea. "Can we at least talk out front for a few minutes?" Brandon asked.

"Not out front. This house has become too well known. You'd better come inside after all." We stayed in the front entry hall while the children ran on upstairs. Brandon glanced at the table where Matt's brass scimitar was lying. "You didn't take it away from him," he commented.

I shrugged. "What would be the use? I haven't exactly been able to shield him from violence, have I?"

I meant to sound flat and rational. Instead my voice came out beaten and weary. I felt tears coming to my eyes.

Brandon made a move to touch me, but then did not. "You were right, I shouldn't have bought that for the kid without asking first. He wanted it so badly, and I thought he had a right." I just looked at him, and Brandon reddened. "Okay, I thought you were being unreasonable. I guess I was, too." He paused. "How are the kids taking what's happened?"

"They're taking it too darn well. We all are."

Again he made an involuntary move; again he checked it. He said good night and reached for the door. I closed it after him and locked and barred it. Then I stood for several moments, my face against the carved wood. I made the rounds of the lower floor, putting out lights, until the house was illuminated only by the moon and stars.

The night was hot, and the scent of flowers was overpowering. I put my foot on the first step to go upstairs, and then I stopped.

When I was little, on hot nights when I couldn't sleep, I used to creep down and sleep on the living-room couch. I didn't want to be in the sitting room here, not all alone, but I did want to be in Mark's study.

I went upstairs and undressed, and put on a caftan I'd bought in Greece. Then, barefoot, I slipped back down to Mark's study. The gold of the icon glowed at me through the dark until I fell asleep.

I don't know when I woke, or what awakened me. Maybe I was dreaming. I felt I was in some small dark place, and I was very hot. I was afraid. Then words from the psalm Rachel had read at family prayer last night blazed in my head.

I will lift up mine eyes unto the hills, from whence cometh my help.

I was awake, and the sense of heat and fear were still with me. I lay there on the sofa, unable to move, and the words of the psalm kept going through my brain.

My help cometh from the Lord . . . He that keepeth thee will not slumber . . . The sun shall not smite thee by day, nor the moon by night.

All at once, call it crazy if you want, I wasn't afraid anymore. I lay there, still webbed in the memory of my dream. And then I heard a sound.

I wasn't even sure it was a sound. It could have been the splashing water in the fountain. But *something* made me rise soundlessly, my bare feet moving noiselessly across the velvet of the Oriental rug, the coolness of the tiles beyond.

My mind was directing me to check the lock on the front door, but something else turned me from it, toward the courtyard. Over toward the table in the entryway.

That's where I was when I saw it. It . . . him . . . I

couldn't be sure whether it was man or woman, the dark figure gliding down the stairs and toward the fountain.

My fingers closed around Matt's scimitar, lying on the table, forgotten in the darkness. Slid it soundlessly behind my back, so that my left hand grasped the sheath, my right the hilt. I moved toward the courtyard, the weapon concealed behind the folds of my dark caftan.

The figure was bending over the curbing of the fountain. It straightened, and in the dim light I could see it was all in black—black robe, black slippers, black kaffiyeh covering head and face. Black gloves.

It looked at me, and the eyes in the blackness burned into mine. I brought the scimitar round and held it hidden in the folds at my right side.

In one leap the figure was in front of me, grabbing for me. I swung the scimitar up. And down. I heard a gasp, and the intruder bent slightly, clasping his right arm.

I held the scimitar straight out in front of me, as though this were one of those horror movies and I were using the cross-shaped hilt of a sword to hold off a vampire.

Neither of us moved an inch.

"I come as a friend." The voice was a harsh whisper, unidentifiable as male or female.

"What do you want?" My voice rasped but I kept it steady. And the sword also. My hands never shook at all.

"Mark Greystoke is held as a hostage by the League of the Sons of the Prophet. They do not wish to harm him. But they cannot let him go until certain arrangements have been made. He is too valuable, and too dangerous."

"All Mark wants is peace."

"The will of Allah is of higher value than a profane

peace. If you wish to see Mark Greystoke alive again, you will come to the Blue Mosque after afternoon prayers tomorrow, for a message to take to your government. Until then you will say nothing."

"Why should I believe you?" I whispered scornfully.

"Before the appointed time you will receive verification that this message comes from the Sons of the Prophet."

I made an involuntary move. Immediately the intruder's right hand came up. But not at me. It knocked the scimitar from my grasp as easily as if it had been a toy. For an instant I thought I heard a sardonic chuckle. Then, with the swiftness of a circus acrobat, the figure leaped for the stairs. Over the railing, onto the first flight halfway up. Up and up, as I ran after, until it disappeared onto the roof.

I stood there outside my room and I shook all over. And then, with all the swiftness and strength that I possessed, I fled down the stairs. First to the door, which was still locked and barred. Then into the study. I slammed the study door shut, locked it, and turned on a lamp.

And I picked up the telephone and I called Brandon.

·18·

Brandon was there in ten minutes. He called out my name as he rang the bell and banged on the door. I unlocked and unbarred and opened it and fell into his arms.

"Tell me," he said. And I did, somehow getting the facts in proper order.

"Have you called the police yet?"

"No! We can't! I told you what he said."

"Then it *was* a man," Brandon said swiftly.

"I'm not sure. Something made me say that." I frowned.

"What? What did you remember?"

I concentrated hard, then shook my head. "I don't know. I think there was something familiar, but it's gone."

"Maybe the police can help you reconstruct it."

"*No police!* You know what I was told."

"The hell with what you were told!" Brandon shouted hotly. "Can't you see you have to—"

"*Don't you tell me the hell with Mark Greystoke's life!*"

"Don't *you* realize that guy may still be in here?" Brandon demanded.

"He couldn't be! From the minute he ran up to the roof the stairs were never out of my sight—" I gasped. "When I phoned you—I locked myself in the study—"

Brandon straightened. "We'd better search, and fast. We'll roust Kamil out to help."

"No. Not Kamil. I'm not sure I trust him." I ran into Mark's study and got the big battery-powered lantern out of his bottom desk drawer.

We started with the study, and progressed to the courtyard, still luminous with moonlight. The kitchen, the storerooms, even Kamil's room—Brandon searched them, while I watched the stairs. Kamil, lying in his narrow bed with his face to the wall, never heard us. Then the sitting room; the dining room. Brandon checked the concealed door to the alley while I waited, the lantern's beam fixed on the stairs.

"Locked," he reported briefly.

We went upstairs. We put no lights on, both in order not to wake the sleepers and so as not to alert the intruder if he were in hiding.

No one was in any of the rooms on the second floor. We checked under beds, in closets and armoires.

On the third floor, the children's doors were locked. I hadn't known they were locking their doors; it bothered me, but I couldn't think of that now. Mine were open, and we searched there. We searched the extra bedroom, and I even tiptoed into Fatma's room and looked around, while Brandon waited in the doorway and Fatma snored. Except for a surprising amount of junk and clutter, Fatma's room held no surprises.

We went up to the roof. Brandon led the way with the lantern, and I followed. My heart was pounding. Brandon swept the beam of light across the rooftop, behind potted plants and shrubs, under and over the garden furniture.

He turned to me, his voice flat. "He's gone. He must have come and gone by climbing the wall up from the roof of the house behind here. Do you know who lives there?"

I shook my head.

"I suppose you can't ask Felicity without arousing her suspicion. Then the police would know."

"I told you we can't bring them in! At least not till after I've gone to the mosque tomorrow."

Brandon looked at me as though I'd lost my senses. "You're not seriously planning to follow those instructions!"

"Of course I am. I have to."

"Not by yourself you aren't. I won't let you."

"Just try to stop me," I said dangerously.

Brandon put his hands on my shoulders as though I were a child. "Meredith, be reasonable. It could be a trap."

"In the Blue Mosque right after prayer time? With all those people there? Where do you think we are, Iran? With a mob of militant fundamentalists waiting to close in on me?"

"How do we know there aren't?" Brandon exploded. "Nobody knows *who* the League of the Sons of the Prophet are! Just because your uncle deserts his family to make a political statement and religious commitment doesn't mean you have to!"

"You don't know what my commitments and beliefs are!" The trouble was, I wasn't sure myself. Not anymore. I sheered away from a precipice and pounced on a word I knew Brandon couldn't argue with.

"Look at the situation logically. Please. It stands to reason, doesn't it, that the Sons of the Prophet wouldn't try anything in a mosque? It's their holy place! And he said—"
I forced my mind back to dredge up the words exactly. "He said 'a message to take to your government. *Until then* you will say nothing.' Don't you see? I'm supposed to get a message to make public. After that I'll *have* to tell the government about the break-in here. Don't you see?"

"What I see is that you could get killed," Brandon said gruffly. And then we were in each other's arms. We didn't kiss, we just held each other tightly for a long time. Then we went downstairs.

We invaded Fatma's kitchen and made coffee, American coffee, which by this time we felt an urgent need for. I laced mine liberally with cream and sugar, and it was probably all that cream that calmed me. We sat at the kitchen table, sipping coffee, and I felt as though we'd scaled Mount Everest and come down the other side.

"I'm staying the rest of the night, whether you like it or not," Brandon said, "so let's not argue." Arguing about it was the last thing on my mind. He slept on the couch in the sitting room next to my bedroom, with the door open so he'd hear if we had any more uninvited guests. Fatma had ten fits when she found him there next morning.

I told her about the intruder, letting her think it was a would-be thief. Fatma promptly went to check out the silverware. None was missing. In her absence Brandon and I discussed whether to tell the children.

"Ignorance is no protection. Besides, do you think you can count on Fatma not giving anything away?" Brandon said, and I agreed. So I told the children what I'd told

Fatma; no less, no more. Matthew was torn between gratification over the role his scimitar had played, and disappointment that he hadn't been there to wield it. Rachel looked sober. I had an uneasy feeling she suspected there was more to the incident than I'd let on.

"You don't have to tell Mom, do you?" she asked.

I shook my head. "I think I'll talk to Mr. Farkas, though. After you kids get off to day camp." Something had to be done to make the roof intruder-proof, and fast. Both Brandon and Rachel looked relieved.

Before we left the breakfast table, the telephone rang. Fatma answered, and came back looking truculent. "That doctor from the church. He wants you. I told him you were eating breakfast, but—" Her complaints grumbled on behind me as I ran for Mark's study.

"Meredith? Have the children left yet?"

"No, I was just about to have Kamil take them—"

"Thank God," Dr. Burlingame interrupted. "Where are you speaking from? Are you alone?"

"I'm in Mark's study. Yes, I'm alone." My throat tightened. "What's happened?"

"My dear, you'd better sit down." Dr. Burlingame cleared his throat as I obeyed, and it came to me that he was, like me last night, forcing every nerve to keep on going. "Less than an hour ago, a van with international license plates roared up to our gates and dumped out—"

The room swam before my eyes. "Not Mark—"

"No, my dear, we can be grateful for that much," Dr. Burlingame said gently. "It was the body of my fellow clergyman, Stephen Althorp. He had been tortured."

God.

"Because of Stephen's connection with Mark, there are representatives of your government and of Interpol, the international police organization, here," Dr. Burlingame's voice went on. "As well as the Stamboul police, of course. The United States government personnel want to speak to you. I have explained why Mrs. Greystoke mustn't be informed. There will be no day camp today, of course. Mrs. Hibborn is on her way to your house now. She will take the Greystoke children home with her for the day. I don't believe any purpose would be served by telling them about Althorp's murder."

"No, of course not," I said mechanically, wondering at the same time how long we could expect to keep it secret.

"I'll ring off, then. Mrs. Hibborn should be with you any moment."

I barely had time to tell the kids the change of plans before she was there. I marveled at her cheerfulness and composure. They left. I told Brandon, swiftly, about Stephen Althorp's murder. Then the "United States government personnel" were there.

I never was too sure exactly what branch of the government they represented, though they showed me their identification immediately. Their right to be there and ask questions was clear. Mr. Murphy was the older one, Mr. Skaggs the younger. Both wore dark suits and military-length haircuts and carried themselves like football players. They asked to see my passport, and I showed it to them. They looked Brandon over pretty sharply.

"I'm Miss Blake's boyfriend. I'm staying here temporarily," Brandon said as though challenging their right to question that. He, too, produced identification.

For half an hour they took me up, down, and through the events since I left home, starting with my reasons for coming in the first place.

"I should think that's pretty clear. My aunt's in a high-risk pregnancy, and her husband isn't here."

"But he was when she asked you to come back with her, wasn't he?"

"And he darn well knew he might be called away any day," I said, trying not to let my voice shake. "Or don't you know what Mark Greystoke's occupation is?"

"We'll ask the questions, Miss Blake," Mr. Skaggs said crisply.

"I can answer some without your asking. Mark's not any kind of spy. Or any kind of traitor, either!"

"No one's suggesting anything of the sort," Mr. Murphy said soothingly. "Now, when was the last time you heard from Mr. Greystoke?"

We went through everything, *everything*. And I told everything—except about last night's intruder.

"Why are you wasting time questioning me?" I burst out at last. "Why aren't you looking for the beasts who killed Stephen Althorp?"

The government men exchanged glances. "There are some details of the Althorp killing that aren't being released to the news media," Mr. Murphy said bluntly. "I must ask you to sign an oath not to make them public unless the White House releases the information."

Brandon and I exchanged glances. Then we both nodded.

It was just like something in a thriller movie. Except it was so *ordinary,* like routine business office procedure.

Routine. That's what we were all going through. It was routine nowadays for people to be taken hostage. It was routine for governments, who'd been doing nothing up till now, it seemed, to step in and tell the families what to do. The families weren't key players in world politics. Even Mark Greystoke wasn't a key player to these men. We were all just incidentals who'd gotten caught up in a deadly game. Even Stephen Althorp was. Correction: had been. I wondered suddenly whether Stephen Althorp, that name without a face, had a wife and children.

Mark Greystoke was just a name, too, to most of the world.

Stephen Althorp had been murdered, Mark had been captured, and Brandon and I, who'd met at the holy place at Delphi, where the prophecies of so much earlier bloodshed had been given, stood here going through impersonal routine. The Greeks would have understood it, maybe. We took oaths, and we signed papers. And we listened as Mr. Murphy laid out the facts in the dry tones of a school lecturer.

"Althorp's body, bound, blindfolded, and gagged, was dumped at the Anglican School as a warning to the Institute for Nonviolent Intercession. The Anglican School is known to be a participant in the peacemaking efforts of the Institute. Among the items found on the body was a photograph of Mark Greystoke taken within the past three days. He is holding a Beirut newspaper of that date in the picture. Also a statement that Althorp's body was delivered to the Institute as proof that Greystoke is being held by the League of the Sons of the Prophet."

◇19◇

I would have fainted if Brandon hadn't caught me. He was right behind my chair, and his arms held my arms rigid. I hoped the other two men had not noticed. The words, *You will receive verification that this message comes from the Sons of the Prophet* were echoing in my mind so loudly it seemed as if the men would hear them.

"That still doesn't explain why you're interrogating Miss Blake," Brandon said coolly.

"We have reason to think the Sons of the Prophet, whoever they are, may make attempts to contact her. Either to ask for a ransom—they still have the journalist, apparently, as well as Greystoke, and they must need funding, since they're a new group—or to spell out other demands."

I didn't move a muscle. I didn't dare risk a giveaway glance at Brandon, but I was certain he had his reactions well in control. "How did Mr. Althorp die?" I asked in a tone as dusty dry as Murphy's own.

"Are you sure—?"

"*Yes,* I'm sure," I retorted harshly. So he told me. In graphic detail, brutal bluntness, that same unemotional flat tone. I thought I was going to throw up. But I didn't

141

move except that my one hand groped for Brandon's, and he took it and held it tightly.

There was a silence. Then Murphy looked at me. "I take it you people have not yet been approached with any demands. When you are, you will report it to us at once."

I nodded faintly.

Finally, they left. Fatma ostentatiously showed them out. When they were gone I groped my way back to the study and leaned against the bookshelves. My mouth was dry and salty. I thought I was going to be sick, but my stomach only retched dryly. I could sense Brandon behind me, watching me in silence, but he didn't touch me. I wanted him to take me in his arms and tell me everything was going to be all right. I wouldn't have believed him if he had.

"You know you have to tell them about what happened last night," Brandon said at last.

"No, I don't."

"If you mess up, Mark Greystoke could get killed."

"He could get killed anyway. He's a lot more likely to if the government gets involved."

"But the creep who was here last night obviously *expects* you to get our government involved. That's the whole point of your picking up their message," Brandon pointed out.

Fatma marched in with a tray of coffee and pastries, which she plunked down on a table, and left, banging the door behind her. We went on arguing, but quietly, because Fatma was undoubtedly listening at the keyhole.

"Meredith, listen to me," Brandon went on urgently. "I know this hurts. You're up against what a professor of mine called the Delphic choice, the same as all the old Greeks were. Remember? I talked about it when I met you. Not just between instinct and reason. Between public duty and private duty."

"Don't lecture me about public duty. That's what got us into the mess of Vietnam."

"Okay, then. Between the good of the many and the good of the few. Sometimes we simply have to make those choices. Because there's just no way to put the two together. And public good has to come first, because otherwise in the end more people die."

"You're trying to tell me I should just stand by and let Mark die."

"No," Brandon said gently. "Only that you may have to. That he may die anyway, and the important thing is to save as many lives as possible. To prevent a war, which could darn well blow up once the news of all this gets out. It's only governments who have any hope of controlling that."

I couldn't answer. The lump in my throat was too large. I leaned my head back to fight off tears.

Brandon poured coffee and brought me some. I ignored it. He stood by the window, sipping his own and looking out through the louvered blinds.

"You're saying it's okay to play Russian roulette with people's lives," I said dully, when I could talk.

"Isn't that what *Mark*'s been doing?" Brandon countered.

Through a fog I heard the front door ring. I dragged myself to the study door and opened it. Anything was better than going on with this no-win argument.

Fatma was just opening the front door for Amina, who bounced in, her eyes sparkling. "Sorry to be so late, I just woke up. We went out after the concert and didn't get home till nearly three! So how was your date, Middle-Eastern style with chaperones? *Oops!*" she broke off gaily, spotting Brandon. Then she saw our faces.

"Meredith—" Amina had no Western reticence about not intruding. She reached out and hugged me. I made a blind gesture to Brandon, and Brandon told her about Stephen Althorp, the official version that was being released for public consumption. And about the intruder, also the official version.

"We were going to call your father, to see what he could do to make the roof intruder-proof."

"Of course." Amina let me go. She went to the phone and spoke to her father at his office, in Turkish. "He'll be right over." She was deeply shaken.

We sat and drank the lukewarm coffee while we waited.

Mr. Farkas came in a dark-windowed limousine. He heard us through, then went through the house on an inspection tour with us as guides, and to the roof. He examined this minutely, then straightened, his voice sharp.

"This person didn't come from the roof behind you, he came from our roof. Look, there are marks of some sort of grappling hook and line, and one of your flowerpots has fallen and been broken. He must have gotten into our garden; the wall around it would be no obstacle to someone trained in infiltration techniques, as the Sons of the Prophet undoubtedly are. There are guerrilla training camps all over in Lebanon and Iran and elsewhere."

"I can't believe this," I whispered.

"Believe it," Brandon said. Amina said nothing. She had sat down, looking as though she were going to be ill.

"How could somebody have gotten in from your place without being seen?" I asked stupidly.

"We were out till nearly three, my daughter and my wife and I, at a benefit for one of the hospitals where Suni practices. It was no secret that we three were going. The servants had the evening off. This person came over our wall, up to our roof, probably by way of the vines that grow on the house—they're very strong—and over here. And left the same way, undoubtedly." He swung round to me. "It was very fortunate that this person did not find you. Did you search the house for bombs?"

It struck me that, although I'd said nothing about my conversation with the intruder, Mr. Farkas took for granted that he was from the Sons of the Prophet, not a thief.

Mr. Farkas made phone calls. A security agent who worked for his company came and checked the house for bombs and listening devices. There were none. Another of Mr. Farkas's employees checked all our doors and windows and protective grillwork, to make sure the house was fast. Mr. Farkas called an ironwork company and arranged for iron spikes to be installed around the edge of our roof and for iron grillwork, the openings too small for a human to squeeze through, to cover the entire roof opening. He also ordered a lockable wrought-iron gate for the stairs leading to the roof. "Mark can always have them removed later, if he doesn't want them. I'll pay the costs, so Felicity need not be brought into this. Please think nothing of it."

I thanked him gratefully.

Fatma and Kamil hovered through all of this. Fatma asked whether the Farkases were going to stay for lunch. They said no. I followed Fatma and Kamil to the kitchen and told them exactly what I thought they ought to know. I also told them what they could do to help—mainly keep watch, and keep quiet.

We ate lunch, late. Rachel and Matt were still at Mrs. Hibborn's. I phoned and asked her to keep them till I called again. I felt guilty imposing on her, then realized she was probably glad to be doing something.

The day went by. The telephone rang, and it was reporters wanting an interview giving our reactions to Stephen Althorp's murder. Brandon got rid of the call quickly. The phone rang again, and it was Felicity, who was cheerful, which meant still in a state of blessed ignorance, and I had to be cheerful back. It was an effort.

The phone rang again, and it was both my parents. News of Stephen Althorp, and rumors about Mark and the other hostage, were raging like bonfires on American TV. I reassured them as well as I could. "More security protection is being installed on the house right now. That's the hammering you're hearing. And Brandon's here."

My parents had heard all about Brandon from my letters. It was a measure of the seriousness of the situation that my father was so glad Brandon was around to protect my safety that he forgot all about being concerned for my virtue.

Finally, in order to get some peace, Brandon simply unplugged the telephones. "Kamil can replug them after we leave for the Blue Mosque. Yes, I said *we*. If you won't let me come in with you, then I'll wait for you at the cafe across the street. I guess you'll be safe enough in the mosque. But you're not going anywhere from there, with anybody, without *me*, and that's that."

I had no desire to argue with him.

We reached the mosque just as the *muezzin*'s call to afternoon prayer was winding down. "We'll go right to the cafe," Brandon said. "You don't want to be in the mosque while prayers are going on." He was right about that. I knew it would be wall-to-wall Muslim men, and that unnerved me.

I entered the mosque, as soon as I saw the worshipers begin pouring out, leaving my shoes on the outer step. Wearing a respectable scarf over my head and a shawl covering my bare arms. Wearing my Western bright-yellow sleeveless dress, so I'd be easy for my contact to spot.

I stood by a pillar at one side of the main central area, waiting. Noticeable but not intrusive. And I waited. Fifteen minutes went by. Half an hour. An hour. Once, a young man in a beard came toward me. I had a sense that there was something vaguely familiar about him. But he turned away, some six feet from me, and went into a side alcove, and began to pray.

My legs were weary. All of me was weary. I leaned against the pillar and the mosque's blue stillness enfolded me. I closed my eyes. *I* was praying . . . not formally, not even in words, but I could feel what the Psalms call the "peace of God that passes understanding."

Eventually, something must have broken into my almost-trance. I came to with a start. The mosque was almost deserted. I looked at my watch. I had stood there for two hours. No one had brought any message. No one was going to.

I made my way out of the mosque, feeling sick at heart.

Brandon was still sitting where I'd left him, at the cafe. Three coffee cups, a couple of soft drink bottles and a decimated plate of pastries told how he'd spent his time. He took one look at me and signaled for a waiter to bring coffee. Strong as it was, and syrupy, I drank it.

"He didn't come," Brandon said. A statement.

I shook my head.

"At least you tried," Brandon said comfortingly.

"That's not much help right now. Maybe you were right. Maybe I should have told—" I groped in my pocket for a tissue. And then I froze.

Something crackled in my cotton pocket, something firm and stiffish, in with the softness of the tissues. I brought them all out, and my hands were shaking.

It was the promised message for the U.S. government, the list of demands to be met for Mark's release.

·20·

I simply sat there, looking at it dumbly. I heard the legs of Brandon's chair scrape, and then he was close beside me, one arm around me, reading across my shoulder.

"You have to take this to those men who were at your place," Brandon said quietly. "What was the head guy's name? Murphy?"

"It won't be any use," I said. "They . . . the government won't meet those terms. It can't."

"Some of these demands are just window dressing," Brandon said patiently. "These people—they're the new kids on the block, proving that they're macho. The main thing they're after's publicity, probably. Some of the things, maybe they can get."

He didn't go on with what I already knew. The U.S. couldn't, shouldn't make some of the promises they were asking for, like requests for major arms. The U.S. couldn't, as demanded, make other countries like Italy and Israel free already convicted Arab terrorists.

"Murphy's still got to see this," Brandon said gently.

"I know. I just . . . I'm so tired. . . ."

"Will you let me take it for you?"

I nodded. I tried to fumble for the card Murphy had given me, but Brandon produced his own. "I'll tell him you're too upset to be disturbed today. I'll run you home in a cab now, and then go see him, and I'll be back to you as soon as I can."

"No, I . . . please." I shook my head. "I have to go to the hospital. I have to make sure Felicity's okay."

Brandon looked at me closely and, blessedly, made no protest. He hailed a cab, put me in it, and gave the driver the hospital address. The cab creaked off. We were in a lot of traffic and had to go slowly. We halted at an intersection with a news kiosk, and I saw posters displaying Stephen Althorp's photograph and a picture of the Anglican School. I didn't try to buy the papers.

At the hospital the receptionist first refused to let me see Felicity, and then when I exclaimed shrilly that I was her niece, said Dr. Koc had been trying everywhere to reach me. "Stay here. The doctor will be right down."

I waited, hands pressed together.

Almost immediately, Suni Koc came hurrying into the lobby. I ran to meet her. "Is Felicity all right?"

"Let's wait until we're in my office, shall we?" She fairly pushed me back down the corridor and into a small room with desk and chairs. "Felicity's in no danger," Dr. Koc said quickly. "But some men from your government have been here trying to see her."

"What?"

"Also, I'm afraid the media have discovered that she's here. You had better sit down, Meredith, we have a lot to cover." Dr. Koc sat down across from me. "The assassination of the English hostage is now public knowledge. I managed to get rid of your government agents, but the hospital administrator and I are sure they will be back.

150

And we're all going to have trouble with the news media. I've been trying to reach you on the telephone for two hours, ever since the information about Mark being a hostage was made public."

"Oh, no."

"I was afraid you might not know," Suni Koc said compassionately. "Someone from the League of the Sons of the Prophet called our main TV news station to take the credit. I couldn't risk the information being sprung on Felicity somehow. I didn't dare wait to discuss it with you, Meredith. I told Felicity myself."

My heart lurched, then sank back in surprised relief.

"Is Felicity—how did she take it?" I managed at last.

"Exactly as you would expect of her," Dr. Koc said simply. "She said she'd been sure for some time now that Mark was being held. That she and Mark had often discussed the possibility of his being taken hostage, and that they had made a pact that if he *were* held hostage, no"—she searched for the correct phrase and came up with a medical one—"no herculean measures would be taken to gain his freedom. She said that would be contrary to everything Mark stands for."

"You mean no ransoming him. No matter what."

Dr. Koc nodded.

The tears were running down my face. I wiped them away with one hand. Dr. Koc went on. "She's very grieved about the Englishman's death, and concerned about the journalist—and about how everything will affect the children. She wants to see you."

I swallowed. "Isn't it dangerous for her to get upset?"

Dr. Koc smiled quietly. "She won't. She won't let herself. Felicity's more than ever determined to save her baby. She's far enough along now that if the worst happens, we have a very good chance of keeping the child alive. Don't be afraid, Meredith."

But I was afraid.

I went into Felicity's room, now guarded by two uniformed officers—whether courtesy of the hospital, Mr. Farkas, the Stamboul police, or the U.S. government, I didn't know. Felicity was lying propped by pillows, her hands folded across her swelling midriff. Her eyes were misty.

"The baby's kicking," she said. "This baby's a survivor, just like Mark. Meredith, come and feel."

After that I didn't have to worry about what to say or not say. We hugged each other, and we wept, but briefly. I had an odd feeling of being underwater, as though we were floating, like the baby was, in a protective sea. We talked about how to handle the media, and the government. We talked about the children.

"They have to be told. Suspecting is far worse than knowing, and we can't take a chance on their finding out from someone else. I wanted Suni to let you bring them to see me, but she won't." Felicity started. "Meredith, I just realized—where are they now?"

"Edith Hibborn's had them at her house since early morning. Felicity, I'm ashamed to say it, but I just can't tell them. I don't know how."

"Edith will tell them. She's the perfect person." Felicity pushed back her pillow. "I think we should ask Edith to stay at the house while I'm gone. Will you do it?"

I nodded. "Mom says to tell you she'll come, if you

want her. Dad will, too. Even Gran and Gramp have offered."

"The last thing we need here," Felicity said fervently, "is my father. Don't let any of them come, please. Not now. The important thing," she went on, pleating the sheet carefully between her fingers, "is to go on living as normally as possible. To fly the flag of faith."

I tried, I really tried. I went to Dr. Koc's office and telephoned Edith Hibborn, who said yes to everything. She would keep the children with her overnight, and bring them home tomorrow along with what she needed for an indefinite stay. After that I rode back home with Dr. Koc in her car, and I was glad I had. The media had, as predicted, turned out in force. Dr. Koc drove her car directly into her own garage, which connected with the Farkas house from the side street, and I went into her house with her, and from there through the alley into mine. I didn't see Amina; she had a headache and was lying down, one of the Farkas servants said.

Our house was still. Fatma and Kamil had all the shutters closed against cameras; the street sounds came through distantly. I called Fatma and Kamil into the sitting room and told them our plans. Felicity's room was to be prepared for Mrs. Hibborn, who was coming tomorrow with the children. I said that everything was to go on as normal, except that they were to admit no one without my permission, talk to no one about the Greystokes or Mrs. Hibborn, and accept no telephone calls for the rest of the day. I would talk to no one.

"No one?" Fatma inquired cynically.

"That's what I said." I was too weary even to talk to

Brandon. I dragged myself heavily upstairs, and Fatma had to shake me before I woke to pick at my dinner tray.

The exhaustion and sense of unreality continued into the next day and beyond. Edith Hibborn came, bringing Matt and Rachel. Before they arrived, fortunately, Murphy and Skaggs came and went. They were furious with me for not having told them about the message from the intruder, for having gone to the meeting on my own. Their dressing down rolled right off me. They wanted to know whether a further meet had been set up. I shook my head no. I didn't even ask them what they were going to do with the list of demands.

Murphy wanted to know how soon they'd be able to question Felicity. I told them to take that up with Dr. el-Faisal. Skaggs said it was pretty strange, Mark Greystoke going off like this when his wife was in such bad shape. I told them about the agreement between Felicity and Mark that no heroic measures like swaps or ransoms should be taken.

"It's easy to say that before you've been kidnapped," Skaggs said sardonically. I just looked at him.

Finally, they left. And Edith Hibborn and the children came. And the Stamboul police, about the intruder. And the media, whom I did not have to let in.

The whole all-too-familiar routine that followed seizure of a hostage had begun. A lot of different governments had their say. And the U.N. And the press. Fanatics on both sides denounced Mark's pacifist stand and his willingness to "dialogue" (that was the institute's word, *dialogue*, not *negotiate*) with the terrorists. They denounced

Mark's being friends with, seeing good in, people on both sides.

Both sides. Us and Them.

Mark was being blamed for his own captivity.

Every time something like this hit the press or airwaves, my parents called. Once my grandfather did, and for the first time in my life I actually experienced "seeing red." The red haze welling up in me literally blinded me. When Gramp started in about how he'd called the White House to demand the president send the marines in to find Mark, I hung up on him.

Matt didn't get angry, and neither did Rachel. They just kept on doing what they did every day, except that they weren't allowed to go out of the house.

All of this shocked me. But what shocked me most was that I found myself hating Mark's dedication and what it had done to us all. It was the very thing I'd always so admired in him, his commitment, his living for the ideals of peace and brotherhood, but now I hated it. Mark had put the greater good—the cause of peace, the cause of saving lives—ahead of Felicity and the baby, and I could not accept it. Knowing Felicity agreed with Mark only made things worse.

And I felt so *tired.* All I wanted to do was sleep. Brandon came over often—he was the only person allowed in except Dr. Burlingame and the Farkases (and Murphy and Skaggs, when they insisted), and it was as though I were in a little glass bubble where he couldn't reach me. I was actually relieved whenever he left. Amina didn't come; she had come down with the flu and was home in bed.

We were all in limbo, waiting.

"What about Meeting Sunday?" Edith Hibborn said to me one day. I looked at her blankly. "My dear, this is the Sunday the Society of Friends is supposed to meet here. You said you wanted to think about it. I can easily have it at my house instead."

"No," I said abruptly. "Let them come." If Edith Hibborn could stand to host a Meeting, so soon after her husband had been murdered, we could, too. Mark was alive. We believed that, didn't we?

I did remember to ask Matt and Rachel whether having Meeting was all right with them, and they said it was okay. I asked what to expect, and Rachel said people just came and sat around in a circle being quiet, and if people felt moved to say anything they did. And afterwards they left. I remembered to ask Felicity, too, if it would be all right, when I saw her on one of my daily visits. I either rode to the hospital with Dr. Koc or Mr. Farkas, or sneaked out through the alley and their back garden to catch a taxi off the side street. Felicity said she was glad that they were coming. On Saturday afternoon, she handed me an audio cassette.

"Play this at Meeting for me."

Sunday dawned scorching hot. The Bosphorus, seen from the roof, shimmered in a haze of heat. At ten o'clock a dozen people arrived for Meeting, in twos and threes, walking through the perennial press and demonstrators like the Israelites walking through the Red Sea. Among them was a tall figure that startled me a little.

"Brandon . . . why are you here?"

"Why not?" he asked reasonably. "Can't I come to

156

Meeting? Mrs. Hibborn said it would be quite all right."

He sat beside me on the banquette, slightly apart but close. Matt and Rachel were across the room, Rachel by Edith Hibborn and Matt with Dr. Burlingame. The silence settled. Then Mrs. Hibborn snapped on her portable cassette player.

"Dear friends . . ." It was Felicity's voice. She was weak, but with an inner luminosity that came through the crackling static of the machine. I could feel tears welling up within me like a great tide beating against a dam, but I could not cry.

Felicity spoke of Mark's convictions and how she shared them, of how they still believed in seeing good in all. After the tape ran out, there was another silence, and then at intervals other people spoke. Sometimes just a few words, sometimes longer. Sometimes quoting passages from the Bible. I didn't know who the people were. I had my head bent, my eyes on my hands or closed. Someone recited Psalm VIII, about "what is man, that Thou art mindful of him?"

ARE You being mindful of Mark, God? something in me shouted. *If not, why the hell aren't You?* I didn't say that out loud. The words came from inner darkness, not inner light.

Why didn't somebody speak for Mark something that wasn't blind faith and platitudes?

And then I heard Matt talking. "My dad's not dead," he said. "I know he's not dead 'cause Dad always said if he were we'd know it. And my dad said even if he were dead he wouldn't be, not really. Not in ways that count. He said he'd be alive in me and Rachel and the new baby, and in

Mom, and in all of you guys. And in everybody who believes the world can still be a good place and worth saving. He said that was the important thing, more important than any of us, to keep believing in the world and in people. And keep working for them. He said the guys he really feels sorry for are the ones who walk around dead inside, or burning up with hate. That's what my dad says."

I looked up; I couldn't help myself. Matt was sitting there, soldier straight. But he was biting his lip, and then he started gulping, and then he sobbed. In a flash Rachel was beside him, hugging him, her shoulders heaving.

All at once my own dam broke.

Brandon's arms went around me. In the silence we walked, he and I, across the room, across the courtyard. Into Mark's study, where the Byzantine icon glowed in the shuttered dimness, and Brandon held me while I cried and cried.

·21·

After that Sunday, life was a little easier. I didn't feel quite so much like a wire wound too tight, and the kids talked more freely. I told Felicity about Meeting, and Felicity looked at me with a little smile.

"I warned you coming to the Middle East could shake you up. This part of the world has a way of altering preconceptions. It intensifies everything that's in us." Her eyes were tender. "By the way, how is Brandon?"

"He's fine. He's been terrific. He isn't even being so . . . supercilious any more."

"And Edith Hibborn?"

"She's a wonder. I don't know how she does it," I said humbly, "all things considered. She's perfect with Matt and Rachel, just the right mix of briskness and compassion. And she keeps them busy. She's teaching them both to do needlepoint." I laughed. "And she's teaching them to tie flies for fishing, because after Mark's back and the baby's born she intends to have you all recuperate, as she puts it, at the Hibborn place in England. It's in good fishing country. And believe it or not, she has the kids making a scrapbook of clippings on what's been happening, for Mark to brief himself from when he gets home."

"I guess there was no use hoping we could keep the

newspapers from the children," Felicity sighed. "This way it keeps their chins up, as Edith would say."

My parents were doing their part, writing daily to me and to Felicity and Matt and Rachel too. Their postage bill must be getting pretty astronomical, I thought, licking the stamps for a fat letter toward the end of August. It was nearly three weeks now since Stephen Althorp's murder. It was two months since Mark had dropped from sight. In a few more weeks Ramadan, the holy month of the Islamic calendar, would begin.

Ramadan, according to the books on Mark's study shelves, commemorated the month in which the Koran, the Islamic holy book, was revealed to Muhammad, and in which his followers had their first major military victory over their enemies. It was a month of fasting, from the *muezzin*'s call before dawn until sunset. The evenings, Amina said, were holiday time. "We eat all night. It's a big time for family get-togethers. The streets are full of people carrying lanterns, and there are street entertainers everywhere." During daylight hours people worked as usual, but life was supposed to be lived with gentleness and restraint.

I wondered whether the coming of Ramadan would be good or bad for Mark and the other hostage. How did the League of the Sons of the Prophet plan to celebrate their holy month?

I couldn't find any clues in Mark's books, and I couldn't ask Amina the Islamic view of holding hostages during Ramadan. Amina was over the flu but it had left her very frail, emotionally as well. She had let me come see her finally, I suspected at her mother's urging, because

Dr. Koc was alarmed that Amina might be sliding into clinical depression. I wondered where Ali fit into all that, but I didn't dare ask. The one time I tried, Amina burst into tears and turned her face to the wall.

Life settled into a waiting mode. The media continued to hang around outside, but in small numbers. I was always careful what I said to them. I knew Mark was an embarrassment to the American government; if I hadn't known it before, Skaggs and Murphy made it plain. I had to be careful about not saying or doing the wrong thing, as they also made painfully obvious.

Now that Edith Hibborn was with us, I was free to be away from the kids. I spent time every afternoon with Felicity. The baby was getting to be a regular little acrobat, she said. We knitted baby things together, and planned a pink nursery, and tossed out silly ideas for names. I read a lot, both escapist paperbacks Dad sent me and Mark's books. I was learning about Islamic ideas and Islamic art. The symbols—a paisley pattern that stood for the cypress tree, the exquisite calligraphy, the eight-pointed stars that represented divine energy flowing out and flowing in—recurred everywhere, in tiles, in pottery, in rugs. "To the Muslim, especially to the Sufi, everything brings us closer to Allah," Amina had told me once.

And I spent time with Brandon. We went to the movies. We went to museums, though not yet to Topkapi Palace. And we went to Santa Sophia, the Byzantine Christian cathedral that was now a museum. "Sophia" meant wisdom, the guide told us.

"In Greek, the word is feminine gender," Brandon told me, chuckling.

"I don't feel very wise lately. Or in control," I said when we were back out in the sunlight.

"So who says you always have to be in control?" he asked reasonably.

"*You* know. I'm supposed to be the glue holding the family together. I can't even hold myself together."

"Stop trying so hard," Brandon said. "Don't try to work on the whole of you at once. Concentrate just on keeping your thumb connected to your hand, for instance. Then move on to the first finger later."

I giggled. But he had a point. I started trying to face each day, and the situations that arose in it, like one of Matt's puzzles. You had the idea of the whole picture, but you didn't try to put it together all at once. You started with the pieces you knew you could fit together.

Brandon signed up for some grad courses in political science at the university here. Back home my classmates had already left for college. Dr. Koc invited us over for dinner on the first night of Ramadan. Everywhere in Stamboul, preparations for Ramadan were going forward.

I still hadn't heard anything from the League of the Sons of the Prophet.

Four days before Ramadan began, an American newspaper printed an interview with a noted scholar of Islamic politics. According to him, if Mark weren't rescued before Ramadan, his fate looked dark. Islamic extremists like the Sons of the Prophet were likely to kill him before the holy month, regarding his death as both a means of having him off their hands and a righteous victory over us infidels in a holy war. "If they didn't think of that before reading this, they will now," Edith Hibborn said bitterly.

Between us, Edith and I managed to see that family prayers that night ended with a positive feeling. But I went to my room afterwards and sat holding the worry beads Brandon had given me for a long, long time. I felt the coolness of the beads slipping back and forth between my fingers, but I didn't see them. I wasn't really seeing anything, just gazing at space between me and the wall.

All at once, on the off-white wall, I was seeing Mark's face.

It was like what had happened before, but more so. I could feel Mark trying to communicate with me. I could feel the dust and stones grinding against his skin, and smell the sweat, and feel the heat. I could see Mark's eyes boring into me. My mouth was dry with thirst.

Mark was *smiling.*

I could hear a voice in my head—not Mark's voice; nobody's voice in particular—saying *the sixteenth of September.*

September sixteenth—the first day of Ramadan.

·22·

I didn't tell anyone about my "vision," if that's what it was.

In the morning, everything was ordinary. We had break-fast in the courtyard. The kids were excited because Dr. Burlingame was picking them up for a day in the country, at the home of old friends of his who had visiting grand-children. Edith Hibborn was planning to spend the day at her own house. "Battening down the hatches. During Ramadan, Muslims have to eat all meals between sunset and sunrise. So breakfast is at an ungodly hour and then the children go out to play at dawn. I want to make sure no balls can accidentally break through our windows." She checked herself and sighed. "*Our*. How long will it take me to get used to saying *my* windows, I wonder?"

"What are you going to do today?" Rachel asked me after Matt had done some noticeable prodding.

"Nothing special. Why?"

"You look kind of shiny, like something nice had happened," Matt said.

"Oh."

"We thought maybe you and Brandon were doing something special," Rachel explained.

"He's coming over, I think." I let them go on thinking

that was the reason for any change they saw. There was a change. I knew, I simply knew, that Mark would come home.

What the first of Ramadan had to do with that, I couldn't guess. Perhaps it was the date on which the U.S. would begin negotiations. But the U.S. couldn't negotiate with a terrorist group that was not a government. Felicity said Mark wouldn't want it done anyway. No matter; I believed what I believed, and I wasn't going to give reason a chance to undermine that faith.

Dr. Burlingame came in briefly before leaving with the children. "Not so many folks outside today. Guess they're all getting ready for Ramadan. No thanks, no coffee, I'm too hot today already. September's worse than August this year." He accepted a glass of fruit juice.

Edith Hibborn left soon after the others did. Brandon came around lunchtime, bearing bags of vegetables and fruit. "I didn't know whether Fatma was having trouble getting to the markets. There aren't too many vultures hanging around out front today, though. Yes, I will stay for both lunch and dinner, if you plan to ask me. I'm getting kind of sick of shish kebab."

Fatma sniffed over his produce, muttering that he'd probably paid too much. I asked her where Kamil was; he was nowhere around. "Those men, they make him go with them, to ask him lots of questions."

Alarm jumped in my throat. "What men?"

"Not Sons of Prophet. They show badges."

So the police were showing interest in Kamil. Or was it Murphy and Skaggs? Brandon and I exchanged glances.

While we were still at lunch the dull roar on the sidewalk picked up. Brandon went to peer through the shutters. "Mailman. I'll bring it," he reported, and a moment later the mail was poked in through the door slot. We always checked it immediately, in case somebody had the bright idea of trying to drop in a bomb.

"No bombs today," Brandon said cheerfully. And then, "Oh, oh. What's this?"

This was a normal size envelope addressed to me by typewriter. The stamp was local, and there was no return address. "Don't touch it, it could be a letter bomb," Brandon said immediately.

"It hasn't blown you up yet, has it?" I scoffed. I held it to the sun. There was a sheet of folded paper inside, and that was all. The sun came right through all of it. I reached for a knife and slit the envelope flap, as Murphy had ordered me to do. He didn't want me to chew up an envelope by tearing it, just in case it had to be examined.

I took out and opened the folded paper.

It was good paper, off-white and letter quality like the envelope. Its message was typed, and what its message said was that I should go to Topkapi Palace tomorrow at two o'clock with the U.S. government's response to the League of the Sons of the Prophet's demands.

"Now you have to give it to Murphy like you should have in the first place," was Brandon's immediate reaction.

I shook my head. "This must be what that message meant—"

Too late, I realized what I'd done. I shut up, abruptly, but Brandon would have none of it. In the end, I told him about what he persisted in calling my "dream."

"It was your own subconscious telling you what you wanted to hear. Besides," he added illogically, "dreams never mean what they seem to, probably just the opposite."

"I don't care!" I snapped. "It helped me." I went to the telephone and called Murphy.

Murphy was otherwise engaged (questioning Kamil?), but Skaggs came right over. He and Brandon were birds of a feather. I should not have opened the envelope. I'd messed up all their lovely fingerprints. He turned the letter this way and that, holding it carefully by the very edges. I stood back and let him have his fun.

"This was cut down from a larger size," he said. "Probably to remove a letterhead. Expensive paper."

"Yes, I know. So what do I do about it? Has the White House 'formulated a response,' I think they call it, for me to take? Or aren't you going to answer?"

"She's not taking it anyway. It's too dangerous," Brandon informed Skaggs on my behalf. Skaggs and I both ignored him.

"I'll get back to you with something. I'm going to have this checked," Skaggs said, and left.

Skaggs didn't come back. Murphy telephoned instead, in the late afternoon. In the morning he would send a sealed envelope to me by messenger, for me to take to Topkapi. I was not to be afraid; I would be safe. I took that to mean he intended to have agents scattered around.

Brandon, who could hear only my end of the conversation, which I deliberately made cryptic, was jumping out of his skin. "You can't go there!" he repeated for perhaps the fifth time in the past hour.

"Brandon, will you please go home?"

"Not till you promise me you're not going. Besides, you invited me for dinner, don't you remember?"

"You invited yourself, as *I* recall. And I don't know *what* I'm going to do tomorrow. I really don't." That was the God's truth. "I'm going up on the roof to read. You can come *if* we don't talk about kidnapping or politics or anything like it. Otherwise, suit yourself." I flounced upstairs with a couple of art books—I made sure they weren't about Topkapi—and Brandon followed.

Edith Hibborn and Dr. Burlingame and the kids came home in time for dinner. Dr. Burlingame stayed, and we all played a game Matt had conned somebody into giving him that day.

When they all left, I told Brandon not to come over the next day, that if he did I wouldn't let him in.

"Does that mean you're going to you-know-where?"

"It means I need time to think!" I retorted.

The next morning, the second day before Ramadan, was even hotter than the one before. We all stayed off the roof. I locked myself in Mark's study, and I read. For some weird reason I could think better when I was reading. I told Fatma to serve lunch early, and as soon as lunch was over I left by way of the alley and the Farkases' garden, taking with me the envelope Murphy had had delivered.

Nobody was following me, and I was glad. As far as I knew, the government people didn't know about our secret entrance. I walked two blocks downhill and got a taxi. It hadn't been hanging around waiting for me; it was letting someone out and I grabbed it. We rode down through the shimmering heat toward the water and the Galata Bridge.

The spires and domes of Topkapi Palace rose before me. It was so beautiful, shimmering in the sunlight. I paid the cab driver and got out—into a sizeable group of Western tourists, to my relief. I went through the entrance. Topkapi Palace wasn't one building at all. It was a whole city, a city of gold and flowers and running water. I moved along the pathway from the entrance, between beds of flowers and long pools with jetting fountains. I walked slowly, knowing the person looking for me would find me.

A young man—he could have been a college student or a young professional—walked toward me. Arab, slight beard, dark suit, something unidentifiable but familiar about him . . . I was sure he was the same man who'd come toward me in the mosque; who'd later slipped the message in my pocket.

I kept on moving forward slowly.

And then, just as we were a few feet apart, someone spoke. It was Brandon, striding forward to say with intimate possessiveness, "About time you got here" and tuck my arm through his where he held it firmly.

I couldn't make a scene; that would blow everything. I tried to slip away but he wouldn't let me. By that time two things had happened. Skaggs was there. The dark young man was not.

Skaggs wanted to know what the bleep-bleep Brandon thought he was doing, and Brandon told him at great length.

"Isn't anybody going to try to find that guy?" I interrupted.

Both of them looked at me. "He'll have been followed," Skaggs said. We were all, automatically, speaking in undertones. Skaggs dashed off to find out something, and the groups of tourists moved around and past us. Brandon and I glared at each other.

Skaggs came loping back. "He got away, thanks to you," he told Brandon coldly. Brandon gave him the Great Stone Face routine. "You'd better go home and hope you get contacted again," he told me. "I'll call you a car."

"Thanks, I'll see Miss Blake home," Brandon said coolly. When I didn't protest, Skaggs left.

"We might as well see Topkapi, since we're here," Brandon said.

I sighed. "Only if you promise—*promise*—not to follow me and try to protect me if I'm contacted again."

He promised sheepishly; I think Skaggs's anger had convinced him. So we saw Topkapi, and it was decidedly better than arguing. It was breathtaking. The gardens, the fountains, the palace buildings, the harem, the weapons room and jewel rooms . . . emeralds the size of baseballs, scimitars covered with diamonds, jeweled crowns sprouting exotic plumes. They were too much to take in.

"The jewels are not merely jewels. They all have meanings," said the guide, and proceeded to explain them.

It was all too much. Too rich, too beautiful, too significant to comprehend. Brandon, I saw, understood. He gave my arm a squeeze and we went out into old Stamboul.

"Want to stay out for dinner?" he asked. I shook my head. "Want to invite—"

"No. Please. I had a lovely afternoon, except for you know what. Now I just want to go home. Alone."

So Brandon flagged a cab, and he got in it with me but made no move to get out when it stopped for me on the side street by the Farkas house.

I slipped in through the Farkases' garden, hearing the muted sounds of voices in their house, the sound of Amina's stereo drifting from the roof. She was playing, not rock, but traditional Turkish music. I waved at Dr. Koc, who was looking out a window, and went through the alley into our dining room.

The house was still. Nobody was in sight. I thought I'd get myself a cool drink and crossed through the dining room into the courtyard. And then, about to circle the fountain, I stopped.

The tropical plants surrounding the fountain basin, the water plants in their pottery containers in the basin, were all as usual. But something had been added. A shining black stone lay there in the water. A stone tied with a golden cord.

·23·

The stone was just the right size to fit through the openings in the roof grille, which we'd thought no one yet knew we had. I stood there, looking at it dumbly. And then, in one swift movement, I scooped it up out of the fountain.

The thing tied to the stone was a plastic packet, plastic like the bags that shops in the bazaar used for purchases. It had been cut down—no shop name was visible—but it was a good heavy grade of plastic. It was sealed shut with heavy tape like plumbers or electricians used.

I carried the whole thing over to the courtyard table and sat down. Methodically, I stripped the tape away. (Skaggs wouldn't like that, I was messing up possible fingerprints, but he'd just have to sort mine out from the others as he'd done before.) I opened the plastic casing.

There was an instant photo of Mark inside, a Mark looking more worn than he had before. And a note in Mark's handwriting. I read it, and then I just sat there, my vision blurred.

Edith Hibborn's footsteps, with their now-familiar squeak of sensible, rubber-soled shoes, came across the courtyard tiles. Her voice, comfortingly matter-of-fact at my shoulder, said, "What's wrong, Meredith?"

Mutely I handed her the message. My vision had cleared enough for me to see she handled it with proper care, touching only the outer edges. She sat down opposite me as she read it, twice, and then looked straight at me.

"What are you going to do about this?"

"I don't know."

She spread the paper out on the glass-topped table and we read it through again together.

Meredith,

I am well and with friends. Has the baby been born yet? I am anxious to see him, but cannot come home until all the negotiations I am here to arrange have been carried out.

Have you received the messages I have sent you? Your orders for this afternoon were not obeyed. I cannot afford to have this occur again. I want a picture of you and the children with my messenger, under a cypress tree in the Old City. Take the children with you to the Grand Bazaar tomorrow afternoon at four. My messenger will find you. Go with the messenger. The photograph is needed to prove that my go-betweens have been in touch with you.

Remember the instructions I have already given you. I insist you follow them exactly. What will be is in the hands of Allah, the all-compassionate.

It was signed *Mark Greystoke,* in writing that, like that in the rest of the note, looked exactly like his, and at the same time different.

"It could be his hand's unsteady from the treatment

he's received," Edith Hibborn said, reading my mind. "It could be he's trying to tell you something."

"You don't think it's a forgery then?"

Edith Hibborn shook her head. "The writing's too much like his. And if it were a forgery, the forger would be copying Mark's *normal* handwriting. He wouldn't risk faking possible side effects of captivity, particularly when they're obviously at pains to make you believe Mark's in tip-top condition."

"What should I do?"

"Well now, that's a question for your own mind and conscience, isn't it? If it were me, I'd seek the inner light before deciding. As for the children, I think I'd let them make up their own minds. They're not so young they don't understand what's involved. They don't live in Eden."

She smiled and left me.

I could hear the water splashing in the fountain, and the distant sounds of the children on the roof. The scent of flowers was almost overpowering. I stared at the message and the photograph, and what I saw instead was Mark's face the last time I'd seen him, on that snowy Christmas. Mark's face alight, intense, passionate in its belief in the methods of Gandhi and Martin Luther King, Jr.

I had to stop thinking about the past and concentrate on now. I took everything into the study and curled up on the sofa. The satin smoothness of the black stone was sun-warm beneath my fingers. I tried to stop my brain from working so it could, as Edith Hibborn would put it, be receptive.

Edith Hibborn's words surfaced. *Maybe he's trying to tell you something.* What was in that letter that could do that? *Has the baby been born yet?* Mark knew it wasn't time. *I am anxious to see him.* Why *him?* Felicity hadn't received the results of her amniocentesis before he dropped from sight. And why the formal *I am* instead of a contraction, there and elsewhere? People only wrote that way if English was their second language; was Mark tipping me off this letter was dictated? There were other things in the message that confirmed that. Orders . . . obey . . . Mark didn't use those words. And Mark wasn't authorized to conduct hostage negotiations; only the governments involved could do that.

My eyes raced on. *Beneath a cypress tree . . .* did that mean something? There'd been something about cypresses in those books on Islamic art that I'd been reading. *Have you received my messages . . .* which messages?

And most of all that last paragraph. *Follow the instructions I have already given you.* That word, *already . . .* as if he wasn't really referring to the directions in this letter at all.

I was coming up with questions, but not with answers, and I knew by now I couldn't force them. I took the letter upstairs and locked it in my jewelry box, and hung the key on a chain around my neck.

The remaining hours of the day passed normally, thanks mainly to Edith Hibborn. She kept a brisk conversation going during dinner. I could feel her gaze on me occasionally, gravely compassionate, but she offered neither sympathy nor advice, and I was grateful. We ate. We played cards on the roof. The Farkases were on their roof, also, and they waved. Or rather, Dr. Koc and Mr. Farkas did; Amina was stretched out on a chaise with her stereo headphones on and her eyes shut.

Darkness began falling. Eventually Edith Hibborn looked at her watch. "Time for prayers and bedtime, isn't it?"

We went downstairs, locking the iron gate to the roof behind us. Doing that was becoming second nature. Following what had also become a pattern, we went to our own rooms and undressed, the kids into pajamas, Edith and I into caftans, before gathering in Felicity's room. Having prayers there seemed to invoke her presence.

It was Matt's turn to read. Instead of going for the shortest passage he could find, he'd picked out Psalm VIII.

O Lord our Lord, how excellent is thy name in all the earth! who hast set thy glory above the heavens.

Out of the mouth of babes and sucklings hast thou ordained strength because of thine enemies, that thou mightest still the enemy and the avenger. . . .

My mind drifted from babes and sucklings (Would Mark be home before the baby was born?) to stilling the enemy and the avenger. The Sons of the Prophet saw themselves as avengers.

When Matt had finished reading, before anybody could start the usual prayers, I put up my hand.

"Something happened today I have to share with you. Something we all have to think and pray about." And I told Matt and Rachel what had been going on, from the beginning, everything they had not already heard, finishing with what happened at Topkapi and the message from the stone.

Edith Hibborn sat quietly and kept her silence. Matt and Rachel looked at each other.

"It's up to you," I said. "I can't ask you to go with me, or forbid it. Or even tell you whether you should or not. I'm not your mother, and Mark *is* your father."

Silence.

"It could be dangerous," I said slowly. "I don't think you'll be in danger, but you could be. We mustn't ask your mother's permission, because . . . well, you know why."

Matt and Rachel exchanged glances again. "Hey," Matt said gruffly, "we're used to danger. Just like Dad is."

"Like you said," Rachel added, "he *is* our father."

"You'd better sleep on it," I said huskily. "We don't have to make up our minds till morning. We don't have to make them up till nearly four o'clock."

There was another silence. Then Edith Hibborn began reciting from memory the Twenty-third Psalm, and we all joined in.

We went to bed and, as on a lot of other nights, I couldn't sleep. The words of Mark's note ran through my mind over and over, raising the same questions they'd raised earlier.

Have you received the messages I have sent you?

. . . Under a cypress tree in the Old City.

Remember the instructions I have already given you.

Then, finally, I remembered the cypress reference. Cypress trees appeared in Islamic art as a symbol of that which bent in the wind, but did not break.

Was Mark simply affirming his commitment to nonviolent resistance? Reminding me of Felicity's promise not to let him be ransomed, rescued by armed force, or used as a political pawn, if captured?

But *I* hadn't sworn. I'd been taught the value of free will, and I'd been learning the hard way to trust my instincts. So whatever happened in the Grand Bazaar tomorrow . . . whatever I *let* happen by going or not going, by what I said or didn't say, did or didn't do . . . was up to me.

·24·

In the morning the kids were still quietly determined to go with me to the Grand Bazaar as Mark's note commanded.

"What do you think? Am I doing the right thing, letting them?" I asked Edith Hibborn uneasily.

"Do you feel God has told you it's right for you to go?" she asked me.

Coming from anyone else, that would have embarrassed me. From her, it didn't. I just nodded.

"Is anything telling you not to take the children?"

"No. That's what worries me."

"Even little children," Edith said gently, "can have their own inner light."

All this theology was getting too much for me.

Brandon called, wanting us to get together. I told him I had a headache, which was more an exaggeration than a lie. "You're going to have a bigger one," Brandon said. "Murphy and Skaggs are on the warpath. They just left me feeling lucky I haven't been court-martialed."

"You ought to feel that way," I said tartly.

"You haven't heard anything more from the Sons of the Prophet, have you?"

I was saved from an outright lie by the doorbell. It was Murphy and Skaggs, and to them I did lie straight out. I didn't think they believed me, but they couldn't shake me. They chewed me out thoroughly for letting Brandon spoil the meet, as if I could have helped it. I didn't bother arguing. Finally they left, after ordering me to stay put in case the League made any further effort to contact me.

Finally I was saved, not by the bell this time, but by Amina's voice in the courtyard. Amina, having a different definition of "personal space" than Americans, simply opened the unlocked door of Mark's study and walked in. She stopped dead when she saw the government men. "Oh, I'm sorry."

"We were just leaving. Goodbye, Miss Farkas." Murphy and Skaggs left.

"Who were they?" Amina demanded when they were gone.

"Government men trying to rescue Mark." But she must have known that; they'd known who she was. No, she'd probably still been down with the flu when they were questioning everyone next door, I remembered. "How are *you?* You look better."

Amina shrugged.

"What's the matter anyway? A fight with Ali?" I asked forthrightly.

"Everything's all blowing up," Amina said vaguely. Then she shivered. "Sorry. I did not mean to use that word. Mama wants to make sure you're coming to dinner tomorrow, all of you. For the first night of Ramadan. We won't eat till close to midnight, you know. The days are for fasting, and we have break-fast, literally, right after sunset."

"Felicity told me. She says the Farkas Ramadan meals

are spectacular. She's sorry she's missing them this year."
We were both taking refuge in commonplaces. Amina was
wandering around the study aimlessly. "I'm surprised
you're not in the middle of preparations," I commented.

"I got out of the house on purpose, if you must know. I
couldn't bear—"

"What?"

Amina shrugged. "Everything."

The fight with Ali must have been a bad one. Or maybe
it had been with her father. "Let's have some coffee by the
fountain," I suggested.

I rang the bell for Fatma. She looked glad to have
something to do. Living in an "infidel" house like ours,
she didn't get to make Ramadan preparations. She was
joining the Farkas servants for theirs, Amina told me.
"She and our housekeeper are great friends."

I linked my arm through Amina's. "We can take our
coffee up on the roof if you'd rather."

Amina shivered slightly. "I've had enough of roofs.
Let's stay down here."

We went to the courtyard, where Fatma was setting a
tray on the breakfast table. "I'll pour," Amina said, hurrying ahead. She looked like she needed things to keep her
busy, so I let her. She handed me my cup and I stood, sipping, as she drank deeply and then set the cup and saucer
down.

Her hand was shaking. Coffee sloshed slightly out of
the cup, off the saucer, onto the papers on the table.

The papers on the table—

I darted forward, feeling cold, as Amina saw what she'd
done and gasped, "Oh, I'm sorry!" She moved the cup

and saucer hurriedly and started drying the papers off with her napkin.

And then she stopped, staring at the off-white paper on which the instructions to go to Topkapi Palace were typed, and the whiter paper of Mark's handwritten message. Her face was as pale as the papers.

She sat looking at them wordlessly. I darted forward. I grabbed them, remembering even at that moment to be careful because they were still damp. I heard the whistle of Amina's indrawn breath. She looked up at me, shaken, and I looked at her.

"You've got to promise me," I said in a harsh undertone, "you'll forget what you just saw. You won't tell anybody!"

"Meredith—"

"Swear!"

We were both talking in whispers because there was no telling when Fatma might appear. Fatma might have read those things already. The government agents would have seen them if they'd come in here—which, thank God, they hadn't. How *could* I have been such a fool as to have left them here after discussing them with Edith and the children over breakfast!

Amina rose unsteadily. "I swear," she whispered. Then she seized my hands. "Meredith, you're not going to go—you *can't* go there, you can't take the children—"

"I've got to."

"But you don't realize—"

"Yes, I do." I looked at her, and the gulf between our cultures, our religions, had never seemed so deep or wide. "Mark's family," I said. "If I don't follow the instructions, they might *kill* him. Can't you understand that?"

"Meredith, I beg you—" Amina's eyes were desperate, tear filled. I steeled myself.

"Amina, go home. And keep your mouth shut! You promised!"

Amina, after a frightened look, obeyed.

I took the papers up to my bedroom and locked them away. The experience with Amina had shaken me. Images of Althorp's mutilated body, of Mr. Hibborn's body, and of that poor legless woman kept coming back to me.

I mustn't let myself think about that.

It was almost noon, and I'd asked for an early lunch. Fatma and I carried the food up to the roof, where Edith Hibborn and the kids already were. After lunch I went to the hospital to see Felicity. It was hard to keep from blurting out things I shouldn't yet, but somehow I managed. Seeing Felicity helped me, hard as it was to guard my tongue. I didn't stay long, for I wanted plenty of time to get the kids and myself ready for the meeting.

I reached the house at twenty after two, through the alley. Fatma stalked to meet me. "This come for you right after you leave."

She handed me an envelope like the one in which the instructions for the Topkapi meet had come, the address typed in the same way. Except this time there was no stamp or postmark.

I whirled on Fatma. "How did this get here? Not through the mail!"

Fatma looked at me coldly. "Street boy deliver it next door. He could not get to door here because of *them*." She aimed an eloquent shrug at the usual collection of watchers outside the front door. "Miss Amina bring it over half an hour ago."

"Thank you." I controlled myself till the kitchen door banged after her, then tore the envelope open.

Same kind of paper, same typewriter, I noted absently. The message was terse. *Meeting changed to Blue Mosque, 3 p.m. Be there.* And instructions for traveling without being seen.

I sprinted for the stairs. Edith and the children jumped up as I burst onto the roof breathlessly. I didn't try to talk, just handed the note to Edith and ran back down. They followed.

Somehow the children got cleaned up and dressed in fifteen minutes flat. Somehow, the three of us got out the back way and nabbed a taxi. Our first taxi—following directions, we took three, traveling to the mosque by a roundabout route.

We pulled up at the Blue Mosque at a minute to three.

We hurried up the steps, remembering to slip out of our shoes and place them neatly, remembering for me to cover my arms with the scarf that I'd caught up at the last minute.

We stepped inside, into peace and dimness. The children clung to me on either side. Rachel glanced up at me anxiously, and I shook my head imperceptibly. I didn't know where to go, but that other time the contact had approached me as I stood by one particular side pillar. I moved that way now. The mosque was almost empty, and no man, young or old, came toward us.

Then, as we passed a pillar, a bent old woman darted out. She was muffled in a veil like some of the fundamentalist women in the side-street markets. She made another sudden dart at me, and grabbed me.

I gasped aloud. With a swift motion, the woman's other arm came up across my mouth. She spun me behind the pillar, and the children with me. Then, before we could make another sound, she released me and, grasping the enveloping veil, opened it just enough for me to glimpse her face.

It was Amina.

·25·

I stared at her, struck speechless. Amina flashed me a warning glance, then bent and spoke to Rachel in French. Rachel gave a brief, comprehensive nod and steered Matt away. They stood with a group of American tourists, out of earshot but in our sight.

Amina had flung the veil up over her head and most of her face again. She swept a frantic look around. "Quick!" she whispered. "There isn't much time!"

"How did you know we were coming here?" Then I gasped, the blood draining from me. "*You! You* sent that message saying the meet was changed to here! *Why?*"

"Never mind that now! There isn't time!"

Things started clicking together. "We've got to get over to the bazaar—"

I swung around, and Amina grabbed me. "*You mustn't go there!* You mustn't take the children! Don't you understand? None of us are safe!"

"*How do you know?*" I drew my breath in sharply. "You typed that letter today, but the one telling me to go to Topkapi was typed on the same typewriter. The same paper. *You're* part of the—" I couldn't say the words.

"No!" Amina whispered. "I swear by Allah! There isn't

time to explain. Just take the children and go home!"
Amina's eyes were desperate.

It didn't make sense. But it had been Amina's typewriter. Amina's house, next to ours. Amina, knowing
everything that went on in our house. Amina, at the same
time so modern and so unexpectedly spiritual. Amina who
felt "like a mongrel," who was European but half Arab,
who loved an Arab—

All of a sudden the missing piece fell into place.

"It's Ali, isn't it?" I asked steadily. "He's a Son of the
Prophet. It was Ali who broke into our house. Who came
over the roof from your house. Ali has known everything
going on at our house, hasn't he? Because you told him!"

One look at Amina's ghastly face told me I was right.

"How did you know?" she whispered.

I shook my head dazedly. "All along . . . I've kept thinking the intruder was familiar . . . but Ali was dressed so
Western the day I met him that I never made the connection. The young man who stared at me here, the day of the
first message; the intruder in our house—it was all Ali!"

"It was Ali here—and in your house," Amina said
starkly. "I didn't know, I swear that! Not till Papa found
the marks of the grappling hooks on your roof edge. Ali's
an expert mountain climber. I was afraid then. I looked at
the edge of our roof, right opposite, and then I knew."

And then she got so sick. A genuine reaction to shock
and horror? Or a way of avoiding facing the truth? Avoiding me—or Ali.

"And Kamil's grandson, our gardener, helped Ali. He's
one of them. Kamil half-knows—he won't let himself—"

Amina swallowed. "Ali wasn't part of Althorp's murder. Or the torture. You must believe me."

"Why should I?" I asked harshly.

"Because I'm here. I may be killed for this. It's in Allah's hands." Amina closed her eyes briefly. "Yes, I told him things, but I never thought—I *loved* him." As though that explained everything. Perhaps it did. "Ali—he's not brainwashed by the ultrafundamentalists. But he does believe in *jihad,* holy war. He believes passionately in causes, and a better world." Like Mark, I thought silently. "He cares about Islamic identity, Islamic values."

That was the little girl who felt lost between worlds talking. I could understand that, couldn't I? "He *believed* in something," Amina went on, almost bewildered. "He *cared.* Most of the people I know in Stamboul don't. The Sons of the Prophet—he told me they were just trying to be heard! Nobody would get hurt! I never thought—*he* never thought—"

"He should have," I interrupted bitterly.

Amina went on as though she hadn't heard. "Getting hold of Mark Greystoke seemed so simple. Such a good way to get attention. It was Ali's idea. He never planned to hurt Mark. But things got out of hand." Amina pressed the back of her hand against her chin to stop its trembling. "What happened to Althorp sickened Ali. But the others—they have some kind of hold on him. They have another hold on him through me. They said they'd kill me if Ali didn't follow through. When he wasn't able to connect with you at Topkapi, they almost killed him then."

I didn't ask how Amina knew all this. "Why are you telling me now?" I asked. "Why are you here?"

"Because I couldn't let you walk into a trap," Amina answered simply. "The—the head of this cell of the Sons of the Prophet—it's not Ali—the last thing he wants is peace. He wants a *jihad*."

"Mark won't let that happen. Not over him. He'll let himself be killed first."

Amina laughed bitterly. "You think they haven't realized that by now? *That's* why I'm afraid! That they'll snatch the children! When I saw Mark's letter today—" She pressed her hand against her mouth. "I know enough about fundamentalism, East *and* West, to know that if the Greystoke family's executed by terrorists, there could *be* a *jihad*."

And Amina and I were just expendable bystanders, or pawns, I finished silently.

"You've got to get out of here," Amina added urgently. "You've got to go home. There may be someone here watching. When you don't go to the Grand Bazaar at four—"

She didn't have to finish. She could be dead. I could be dead, if they found me on the streets. And the children—

"What about you?"

Amina shrugged, that fatalistic Middle Eastern shrug. "It's in the hands of Allah."

"You know if I go home I may call my government and tell them everything."

Amina didn't answer, but our eyes met.

I took a deep breath. "I'm not going home, Amina. I'm going to the bazaar."

Amina drew her breath in sharply. "You must not."

"Yes, I must. But I'm not taking the children."

Amina's eyes showed she understood. She waited, accepting, while I considered. I had to get the kids back home, but how? If Amina had spotted us here so easily, certainly Ali, or any of the Sons of the Prophet, could have, too.

I looked at the children. They were already barefoot, their sandals left properly at the entrance of the mosque. Their feet were stained from the street's heat and dust. They were deeply tanned to start with, and Matt had his father's eyes. They looked like Stamboul urchins.

"You'll be safe with Amina," I whispered. "Keep your eyes down." They nodded. Neither of them had said a word through any of this. There had been no need; they'd understood the situation and I knew it.

Amina looked at me with pleading eyes. I shook my head. Her eyes dulled. Suddenly she leaned forward and kissed me on both cheeks. Then she took Matt and Rachel by the hand, and I faded behind the pillar as she led the children slowly off.

I waited several minutes, and in those minutes I prayed. Hard. It was a mixture of *Bismillahi ar rahman ar rahim* and *The Lord is my shepherd* and *The Lord shall preserve thee from all evil* from the Hundred and Twenty-first Psalm, which I'd been saying to myself a lot lately for Mark's sake. And snatches from every prayer of childhood that I'd ever known.

Snatches of so many things were crowding back on me . . . things Felicity had said, and Mark, and Gramp. Things Brandon and I had talked of. Even scenes from Greek plays, and Delphi, closed in on me. Because that, for me, was where all this had started. With Brandon and his talk about the "Delphic choice" between intuition and reason, between public and private duty.

And finally, I knew what I believed. Brandon had a blind spot, I thought. Because intuition was a form of reason. I should have known that anyway, from Gran's samplers. The need to accept what can't be changed and let go of it; to recognize what can be changed and build on it; to not be distracted by worrying over what can change itself.

I would think about that later. Right now I was going to keep my "meet." Because that was the thing that *I* could do. I couldn't personally save Mark's life, or free him, or save the children's lives (and perhaps my own). What I could do was meet Ali or whoever, and try to find out more. I could decide whether to turn over that information to the government, or not. I could try to stop Ali — one way or another.

As soon as I'd left the mosque, I bought a knife to take with me. A strong knife, not a toy like Matt's lightweight scimitar. I wasn't sure whether I could use it, but I thought I could if the need arose.

Because the choice wasn't always clear-cut between violence and nonviolence; that was too simple, and I suspected Mark knew that too. I tucked the knife into my handbag. What I was sure of was that I had to be involved. Whatever the cost. Otherwise I'd be collaborating in the wrongs I saw going on, just as surely as Ali had done.

◇26◇

It was not far from the Blue Mosque to the Grand Bazaar. I walked; no one bothered me. And as I walked, I thought. No, not thought, exactly; I ran the worry beads between my fingers and let windows in my mind stay open.

By the time I reached the Grand Bazaar I knew what I would do.

I didn't go inside. I stood by the entrance, intently watching. At last I saw Ali coming along the sidewalk.

He was swinging along, not on his guard or looking for me, since he expected me to be inside in the bazaar's dark corridors. So I had the advantage.

I moved forward surreptitiously as he came toward me, not really seeing me at all. He brushed past me, "invading my space" without even being conscious of it. As he did so I grabbed his right wrist with my left hand.

He checked, startled, and looked at me for the first time. I saw impatience change to surprise and then alarm. He recognized me. I looked him straight in the eyes.

His eyelids flared, and he jerked his right arm, trying to get free. I hung on, digging my nails into his wrist.

"Oh, no, Ali. You don't want to be seen running from me like a coward. We *will* be seen, won't we?"

"I don't know what you mean."

"Listen to me, Ali. I don't think your friends would have trusted you to kidnap three people on your own today, not after you messed up yesterday at Topkapi. Maybe they'll even make you one more martyr for the cause. Because I didn't follow your directions. Mark Greystoke's children didn't come here with me."

It was so weird. There we were in front of the Grand Bazaar, speaking in whispers, and nobody paid any attention. Life just flowed on past us. In movies, I'd seen scenes of spies meeting in public, and had not believed them.

"What do you want?" Ali asked hoarsely.

"To talk. That's all for the moment. Now are you going to come with me to that bench over there, or do I leave you to tell your friends you failed to convince me?"

I could feel the resistance oozing out of Ali's wrist, which I still held. I kept on holding it as we crossed the grass and sat down.

"How did you know?" Ali's face became ugly. "Did Amina—"

"Leave Amina out of this! She didn't have to tell me. I could guess."

"And you came here anyway!" Ali gave a sneer very like the ones Skaggs used for intimidation. "Why?"

"To make you tell me where Mark Greystoke is! I know he's somewhere very close to here. Why? So the Sons of the Prophet can release him if their demands are met? You know they can't be. Or so you can kill him on our doorstep the way you killed Stephen Althorp?"

"You're crazy!"

"No, I'm not," I said steadily. "Mark's not in Lebanon. Maybe he never got there. He's not there now, because he had to be close enough to Stamboul to be forced to write that note, after our meet at Topkapi was blown, in time for you to drop it in our fountain before I got home from Topkapi. Weren't you lucky Brandon made me hang around there awhile for sightseeing?"

"I'm not going to tell you anything."

"Oh, I think you are," I said coldly. "Because when you don't produce the kids this afternoon, your buddies will probably take revenge not just on you but on Amina. You wouldn't want that, would you?" He didn't answer, but something flickered in his eyes. "And because I know who you are now. Before this, the Sons of the Prophet have just been shadows. That's been their power. Nobody knew who or what they were dealing with. They will, as soon as I blow the whistle."

"Greystoke will get killed, you know, as soon as all this is known."

I shrugged. "He's prepared for that. He's been pre-pared all along. He'd rather die than be used as a pawn in a political struggle or a holy war. That's what none of you have understood. That's *his* power."

"What makes you think you'll live to blow the whistle?" Ali asked me softly.

"What makes *you* think Islam has a monopoly on martyrs?"

Our eyes locked, as Amina's and mine had locked in the Blue Mosque. Ali made a slight move, and I gripped his arm more tightly. "Let's get this over with. Are you going to tell me now, or shall we get a cab to the American consulate so you can try to work a deal with the U.S. agents? Maybe you could manage to save your skin. Or are you really set on a holy bloodbath here?"

His eyes challenged me. "It's your call," he whispered softly. I thought I heard a faint rustle, saw a faint movement, behind him among the passersby. It could be the Sons of the Prophet. Or it could be—

I let out a sharp whistle between my teeth.

Immediately, Murphy and Skaggs, each with back-up and all holding guns, came racing from two directions. And from a third came Amina and her father!

It was all over in an instant. A minute later, Ali was handcuffed and in an unmarked car. Mr. Farkas was holding me, and I was shouting, "*Mark!* You have to find Mark quickly, before—"

"We know. We've already located the house," Skaggs called abruptly, climbing into the car beside Ali. I drew back, not knowing whether to laugh or cry. And Amina—

Amina, her face ghastly pale beneath its makeup, jerked open the car door on Ali's side and looked straight at him. "I could live with your being a fanatic," she said coldly. "I could even live with your using me like you did. But I can't live with your being a murderer! You shame the name of Allah!" And she spat right in his face.

·27·

Bismillahi ar rahman ar rahim. It was the middle of October, the last night of the holy month of Ramadan. In two more days, I would be flying home. Tonight was the feast of *Id al-Fitr,* the great festival that ended the fasting of Ramadan, and we were celebrating at the Farkas home.

All of us were celebrating—Dr. Koc and her husband; Amina, looking wan but steadfast; Matt and Rachel and I. And Brandon, and Edith Hibborn, and Dr. Burlingame. Even Fatma and Kamil were celebrating somewhere in the house with the Farkas servants and members of their families.

And Mark. And Felicity. And the baby.

We had a lot to celebrate. Ramadan. Mark's return. The birth of Stephanie Meredith Greystoke (Stephanie for Stephen Althorp) three days after Mark got back, just in time to be Felicity's labor coach as scheduled. Stephanie was five weeks premature, but healthy, and she'd only come home from the hospital yesterday.

So much had happened, too much for any of us to quite understand yet. But some things had become clear.

Mark had gone into Lebanon, but his meet with Althorp's captors there had apparently fizzled out. So he'd started back to Istanbul again, still with his Arab contact.

What he hadn't known was that that contact was a member, not of the recognized negotiating party, but of the League of the Sons of the Prophet. It was a new, nationalistic group that had been recruiting among youths in the streets (like Kamil's grandson, now under arrest) and on college campuses among student radicals (like Ali).

Somewhere between western Turkey and Stamboul, the Sons of the Prophet had had a great idea, triggered by the rumors that Mark was a hostage. They'd decided to hang on to Mark Greystoke; he was internationally known as a reconciler, not political, and if they played their cards right they knew they could turn him into a hero like Gandhi or King and then no government would want to be embarrassed by his being killed. They'd get publicity, and maybe some of their demands, and in the end they planned to let him loose and pass themselves off as the good guys who saved him from his Lebanese captors. Only a few things went wrong.

One was that Mark's principles were so deeply ingrained that he was like a cypress tree—he could bend, but not be broken. He was willing to die for peace. Another was the young man who'd become leader of the Sons of the Prophet, the third man I'd seen in the street market. Once he had power, he turned out to combine the most fanatical elements of the Ayatollah Khomeini and Karl Marx. By the time Ali discovered that, he was in too deep to break away. Even if he wanted to; I wasn't convinced about that, but I pretended to be, for Amina's sake. The only way Amina was managing to live with all this was to believe that Ali kept on, after things got bloody, in order to save her life. It could be true, I thought, remembering the flicker in Ali's eyes.

The leader had had Stephen Althorp and the kidnapped reporter brought from Lebanon (the reporter turned up untouched, the day after Mark's release, wandering in the desert of eastern Turkey). Only things hadn't gone as expected—we hadn't started denouncing the U.S. government for not rescuing Mark, among other things—and Althorp had been killed to hurry things along.

For Amina's sake, we were all glad there was proof that Ali had not been on the premises when Althorp was murdered. That was a point in his favor, when his case came to trial. The location of those premises was not.

The location had been an old wooden *yali,* one of the famous nineteenth-century "summerhouses" built by wealthy Stamboul families along the Bosphorus. One owned by Dr. Koc's family and long boarded up but used for occasional picnics. Mark and Felicity had been guests at one of those picnics a few years earlier.

"I recognized it when they took my blindfold off so I could write that note," Mark said as we ate the *Id al-Fitr* feast. He helped himself liberally to the *pièce de résistance,* a whole lamb stuffed with dried fruits, almonds, cracked wheat and onions, roasted till it was tender enough to eat as we were eating it, with the fingers of our right hands. We hadn't had a chance to get many details before tonight, what with so much going on. Not just the baby, but medical exams for Mark and endless questioning by authorities of all varieties, not to mention endless questioning by reporters. "But I couldn't think of a way to tip you off that wouldn't put the Farkases in danger."

"I had enough trouble figuring that letter out," I answered, grinning.

"One thing I still don't understand. How did the Sons of the Prophet get to use your *yali?*" Dr. Burlingame asked Dr. Koc. "Felicity says she'd forgotten you even had one."

Everybody looked embarrassed. "That was my misdeed," Amina said steadily. "Ali and I . . . I took him there in the spring. We used to meet there. Only then—" She pressed her hand against her chin. "Ali said we must not go there anymore. That it was not honorable."

Because he had Mark hidden there by then, I thought cynically. Amina had finally figured that out.

It was only after she was sure that Ali was involved in Mark's kidnapping that Amina began to suspect Mark was being held in the *yali.* She'd remembered what I told her about the background noises in our mysterious phone calls, and she'd connected them with the horns of the riverboats going by the *yali.*

It was true, what I'd heard . . . terrorist situations could scramble your brain, turning emotions and reasoning inside out, making you hard. But not Felicity, not Mark, I thought humbly. I felt Mark smiling at me, and I smiled back.

"There's one thing I'd like to know," Mark said slowly, "now that we're letting everything hang out. What made you do what you did at the bazaar? What did you expect?"

"I don't know," I answered honestly. "It was my inner light guiding me, I guess. Of course, Brandon would call it my subconscious. I just . . . knew I had to do what I believed in, just as you did. And I finally felt as though I were beginning to know what I believed. That people have to stand up for what they believe is in the greater good, no matter what the cost." I glanced at Mark, then away. "Like you do. We don't always agree about what the greater good is, but it's the same idea."

"We're on the same wave length," Mark agreed gravely. There was the faintest twinkle in his eyes as he glanced at Brandon briefly. Brandon threw his hands up.

"Okay, okay! Call it conscience, or intuition, or subconscious, or whatever. *Something* operates 'faster than a speeding bullet.' You don't need to convince me!"

I smiled. "I had a pretty good idea Murphy and Skaggs were skulking somewhere near," I went on. "If only because they'd been so mad at me for keeping the first message secret, and blowing the Topkapi meet! If they hadn't been—" I didn't finish. I let my breath out. "I had no idea," I said in a low voice, "that Amina'd do—what she did."

"I did what I had to," Amina whispered simply.

For a minute we all were silent. We all knew what that had been. Amina had taken Matt and Rachel not home, but to her father's office, and told him everything, including her suspicions about the *yali*. And *he'd* called the American Embassy, which had taken over, sending Skaggs and Murphy to my rescue.

Did Amina still love Ali? I glanced surreptitiously at Amina's drawn face and knew I could never ask her.

"Enough of this!" Mark lifted his glass of fruit punch as the servants cleared the table and began serving pastries.

"This is a celebration, remember? We're all alive, and this is the last night we'll be together for quite a while!"

In a few days I was going home. My parents still thought I was too young to go away to college, but there was a college in Bloomington. Maybe I could take a few courses.

Brandon was flying back to the States with me, to my father's mingled relief and concern. Relief because I wouldn't be traveling alone; concern because Dad had figured out that Brandon was four years older than me. Particularly in view of the fact that Brandon was planning to start his graduate studies, in East-West relations, at the University of Chicago. Chicago was only an hour away from Bloomington.

Amina made an effort to pull herself into the holiday mood. "Many of us will be together for your Christmas." She turned to Mark. "You all are reaching the States for your visit by then, aren't you? Did you know Meredith has invited me to spend the holidays with her family? So I'll see you there." Dr. Koc and Mr. Farkas, after thinking things over, had concluded Amina would recover best from the shock of Ali and everything if she were worlds away. She'd been accepted at the University of Chicago as a second-semester freshman, and would reach America in time for Christmas. Maybe I can persuade my folks to let me start at the U. second semester, too, I thought hopefully.

"Will you be in Bloomington for Christmas, too?" Matt asked Brandon with enthusiasm. I blushed, Rachel hissed to Matt to shut up, and Brandon only said noncommittally that he didn't know.

He didn't push the subject further till we'd left the Farkas house and gone back next door. Mark and Felicity tactfully let us go up to the roof alone to watch the dawn.

"This is one of the things I'm going to remember most about Stamboul," I murmured dreamily. "Watching the sun on the dome of Santa Sophia and the Galata Bridge."

We could hear the *muezzin*'s call to prayer, faint and musical. Brandon's arms tightened around me. "I'm going to miss the *muezzins*," I said.

"What else?"

"The Blue Mosque. And the fruits. And the pastries. I'm *not* going to miss the coffee. Or the smells in the bazaar."

"Go on," Brandon said. "Isn't there something else you're going to miss?"

"Not arguing about the superiority of reason, I'm not."

"What about Christmas?" Brandon asked. "Irrational, a lot of it, I admit. But everybody should be home for Christmas. All the songs say so. At least at somebody's home. Are you going to invite me?"

"That's more than two months away. Are you sure you'll still want to come by then?" My pulse beat harder.

Brandon gave that slow smile. "Oh, I think that's a rational assumption."

"You may get bored. Bloomington's kind of a small town."

"I'm sure we'll think of something to do to fill the time." His eyes glinted. "If worse comes to worst we can always have another instinct/reason discussion."

"Oh . . . I think we can find better things than that to do," I said.

About the Author

Norma Johnston has, under eight different names, written over sixty novels for young adults. Her books have included the acclaimed Keeping Days series of novels, *The Potter's Wheel, Gabriel's Girl,* and *The Watcher in the Mist,* which was an International Reading Association — Children's Book Council Children's Choice selection. Her most recent book was *Return to Morocco.*

Readers can write to Ms. Johnston c/o Dryden Harris St. John, Inc., 103 Godwin Avenue, Midland Park, NJ 07432.